Praise for the Sons of Amber

"This is a WONDERFUL story and I simply loved it! ...Zeke and Angela are two characters who are thoroughly written, and I fell in love with them as they did with each other." - 5 Cups from Coffee Time Romance

"Not only do these Sons of Amber make fantastic romantic heroes, they are also men to admire and you hope that each one finds their very own heroine." - 5 Angels from Fallen Angel Reviews

"In the second edition of this series, we see more of Michael, the title character who we first met in Ezekiel. As intriguing as he was in that first story, he blew my socks off in this one! He is just the right balance of Dominant Alpha Male, caring, considerate man, and conscientious leader." - 5 Klovers from CK2S Kwips & Kritiques

"...an intensely passionate story of discovering love. I loved everything about this book, it has characters that not only grow on you but also make you sit up and take notice of them, while depicting a scenery that takes on a life of its own." - Ecataromance Sensual Reviews

"Bianca D'Arc possesses a special talent for creating a futuristic world... Her grasp of the scientific background is excellent; and her characters are especially well-drawn and three-dimensional." - The Romance Studio

Published by Phaze Books
Also by Bianca D'Arc

Sons of Amber: Ezekiel (eBook)

"King of Swords" from
Fortune's Fool

Sons of Amber: Michael (eBook)

PHAZE
Cincinnati, Ohio

www.Phaze.com

Sons of Amber

Ezekiel & Michael

a collection of science fiction erotic romance by

BIANCA D'ARC

Sons of Amber © 2006, 2007, 2008 by Bianca D'Arc

Cincinnati, Ohio

A Phaze Production
Phaze Books
6470A Glenway Avenue, #109
Cincinnati, OH 45211-5222
Phaze is an imprint of Mundania Press, LLC.

To order additional copies of this book, contact:
books@phaze.com
www.Phaze.com

Cover art © 2008 Stella Price
Edited by Kathryn Lively

ISBN-13: 978-1-59426-895-3
ISBN-10: 1-59426-895-1

First Edition - March, 2008
Printed in the United States of America

10 9 8 7 6 5 4 3 2 1

Part One: Ezekiel

Prologue

Dr. Amber Waithe looked at her sons with pride. They were all the finest specimens of manhood, most of whom clearly exhibited the dominant and protective genes she'd labored over, and some showing signs of being risk-takers and pioneers. They were all physically strong, but were mentally superior as well. They had high-level intelligence and steady personalities, the best she could design.

And they all bred true.

Each and every one of them was totally immune from the jit'suku virus that so cursed many others. The jits thought they had struck the final blow in the Unwinnable War, but they were wrong. It was Amber and her sons who would prevail in the end. The jits had not ended humanity within three generations, as they planned when they had been defeated at Markesh.

Their doomsday weapon-the virus intended to attack the human reproductive system-had ultimately failed. Not solely because of Amber, though her genetic research did have a lot to do with the recovery of the human race, and would well into the future. No, it was their failure to really understand human reproduction in the first place that had been their downfall.

Amber's research revealed their grave miscalculation. jit genetics, while closely resembling humans in other ways, actually defaulted to the male. By contrast, Homo sapiens generally defaulted to the female. The jit virus, which had mutated through the human population to eventually infect the jit'suku themselves, was designed to kill off all male humans-even those still in the womb. It was a point of jit'suku honor that they did not make war upon women, but their bioweapon was more deadly than they'd thought and it did kill some women, sickening and scarring many others with the result that they became infertile as well.

Humans were just different enough from the jits in the microscopic ways that counted, though the vast majority of human children born after the virus attack were female. With Amber's help, and the few males who were immune or otherwise able to avoid being infected, some male children were born to perpetuate the species, but not enough to keep it viable. Which is where Amber's sons had their purpose.

Designed in the lab, they were sex machines with high intelligence. Add dominant alpha male traits, killer physiques, and the skills to match, and they were all completely immune to the jit virus. She had carefully planned the first generation of her boys so they would breed ninety-seven percent male offspring. Successive generations would equalize over time to the human norm of about fifty-fifty, but by her calculations, that would be well into the recovery of the species as a whole. They would have done their jobs by then, and the future generations' genetics would normalize.

All as she had planned.

Chapter One

Zeke looked about and grimaced. The dark earth beckoned to him, but he couldn't drop yet. He had to find shelter before the sun rose higher, or he would burn to a cinder on this godforsaken rock.

Zeke had more than his share of stamina. It was a gift of his genetics. Designed and raised by Dr. Amber Waithe and her team of geneticists, he knew he had a mission in life: to spread his seed far and wide, bringing his fertile offerings to every woman who would have him. By the Maker, he enjoyed his job.

But even his enormous strength was taxed by the huge binary stars that were just a little too close to this dry, arid planet. Too bad his Risker's nature had brought him here but he was usually able to roll with the punches. Riskers had to be able to deal with the results of their actions, and he was one of the best at making lemonade out of lemons.

This time, however, he might just die for his troubles. The suns were rising all too quickly, and he was caught out in the open. He took one last, long, weary look at the suns and kept on trekking. Minutes, or maybe hours later, he felt himself fading under the onslaught of oppressive heat and strong solar radiation. He saw the dusty ground rush up at him as if from a distance, then he knew no more.

* * * *

Zeke woke hours later, feeling a cool wetness on his face. He had to be hallucinating, but he didn't feel the merciless suns pounding down on him anymore. No, instead he felt the coolness of earth, the scent of dirt and dampness in his nostrils, as if he were in a cavern. Cautiously, he cracked one eyelid just enough to see.

There was a woman at his side, mopping his brow with a damp cloth. The suns were blessedly absent. He was in a chamber somewhere underground if he didn't miss his guess. He had no idea how long he'd been out or who had saved him. Somehow, they'd transported him to his present location-wherever that was. He searched his memory, but didn't remember anything after passing out in the heat of the twin suns.

"Sister, he wakes."

The treble voice came from somewhere off to his left as the cool hand abruptly lifted from his brow. He wanted that cool, wet cloth and gentle touch back. Badly.

"Are you well, brother traveler?"

The soft voice caressed his senses, and he opened his eyes to behold the most beautiful woman he had ever seen. His savior was an angel, he was sure, her face, heart-shaped and lovely, even devoid of the usual cosmetic alterations women of the upper classes habitually made. No, her face was pure and natural, one hundred percent human female. She was soft, slightly rounded, and perfect.

Her delicate eyebrows drew together in concern as she studied him. Her hand touched his face once more with the cool cloth and it was bliss.

"Are you well, brother?"

"Just keep doing that." His voice was a deep rumble. "Your touch is comforting."

He looked up in time to see her slight blush, but she continued stroking his brow with the wet cloth. A hesitant smile lit her curvy lips. Lips he suddenly longed to kiss in passion.

But his body was telling him something was definitely wrong. He felt achy all over and weak. He had never felt so feeble before in his life.

"What happened?"

His angel spoke as she tended to him. "I found you on the surface at midday. I don't know where you came from or how you came to be on the surface at such a dangerous time."

"Ship crashed." His strength was waning and he damned the weakness that stole over him. His eyes drooped with weariness.

"You came from the stars?" He heard her hesitate and his eyes reopened. He read fear in her gaze now and he didn't like it. "Are you human?" She seemed to steel herself for his answer.

"Be at ease, lady. I'm as human as you. I'm one of the Sons of Amber, designed to rebuild the human race."

Usually all he had to do was mention his illustrious mother and all doors were open to him. Males were that rare. Breeder males even more so. But this attractive little woman did not seem to understand what his words meant.

"You're not jit'suku. That's good." She seemed to want to reassure herself. "It's just that we have not seen anyone from the stars in many, many years. Our Order selected this inhospitable planet as a retreat when the war came too near our home on Espia. Our elders cut off all communication with the outside so that we might hide from the jit'suku."

"Then you don't know what happened?"

His angel shook her head, and he noticed the other women drawing near to listen in. He had to tell them, but he was so damned tired. Still, he could give them the bare bones at least, before his strength gave out completely.

"We defeated the jit'suku at Markesh, but they released a virus that infected just about everyone. It killed most males and caused what few babies that were born to be female. They intended to wipe out humanity within three generations," he paused to breathe through the fatigue that plagued him, "but Dr. Amber Waithe genetically engineered a group of male children that were immune to the jit virus. I'm one of them."

The angel sat back, looking stunned.

"Did you hear, Sister Angela?" The other little nun was back now, moving closer on his other side. She was younger than his angel, but cute as a button.

For the first time in his life, he realized he was looking upon an eligible human female without any trace of lust. That thought had him rocking back on his heels, figuratively at least. Perhaps it had something to do with his illness, but no, he wanted his angel as much as he ever wanted any woman.

Actually, more so. He didn't think he had ever wanted a particular woman this badly.

The realization confused him, but he was too weak to sort through it now. He decided to concentrate his energies on getting well first, then he would bed his angel and figure out why she was so irresistible.

"I heard, Sister. We must tell Mother Rachel."

"I know already, children. Be at ease." A new female voice floated through the chamber to him, coming closer. With it came a fragrance of flowers and earth, and a beautiful, slightly older woman stepped into his line of view. "Your arrival was foreseen. Be welcome, Son of Amber. Can you tell us your name?"

He didn't know why, but he wanted to tell this lovely older woman whatever she wanted. He would reveal all his secret plans, if she but asked, but she only wanted his name. That he could give her before his strength failed.

"Ezekiel."

"Be welcome, Ezekiel." She placed her hand on his forehead and he felt a peace he'd never experienced before wash over his senses. "Rest now and recover."

* * * *

That was all he knew until he woke a full day later. The angel was gone but the cute little nun was at his side, watching him with wide, almost frightened eyes. He tried to sit up, but found himself in too much pain to move very far.

"Oh please, do not move, brother."

"What's wrong with me?"

"'Tis the aftereffects of the *tessla* we gave you to deaden the pain. Your head will clear in a few moments, but you must lie still. It will take much longer to be free of the *tessla* if you do not." She moved back as he resettled, then went to the doorway, calling for someone before returning to his side. "Sister Angela will come shortly. She will want to see how you're feeling."

"Who is Sister Angela?"

The young girl giggled. "I'm sorry. The other woman who was here when you woke last. That is Sister Angela. She is one of our most talented healers. It was Sister Angela who set your leg."

"My leg?" He tried to lift up again but sat back abruptly as the room began to spin.

"Your leg was fractured." A new voice sounded from the doorway. Zeke swiveled his eyes up to see the angel who had tended him. She moved softly into the room, her strides brisk but feminine in a way that caused his gaze to linger. "But it is knit well now. After the *tessla* wears off, you should be ready to sit up for a bit."

"You're Angela?" She nodded, and he liked the blush that came over her pretty face as she moved closer. "Thank you for tending my injuries. You, too." He turned toward the younger girl with a small smile. "I didn't get your name."

"I'm Agatha." The younger girl blushed, too, though it didn't have quite the effect on him that Angela's blushes had.

"Thank you, Agatha. You both have been angels

of mercy in my hour of need."

Angela moved closer. "It's part of our calling."

For a dreadful moment the pit of his stomach fell, as if he were in free fall. "Are you part of a religious community? Are you, uh, nuns or something?"

Both girls chuckled and it somehow reassured him. "We're part of a fellowship, but it's not religious in nature. Our ancestors banded together because of their shared abilities and left the homeworld as a group."

"Then you're not under any kind of vows or anything, right? You're not, uh, celibate?"

The blushes returned even fiercer than before, and both sets of feminine eyes darted away, but there was excitement in the air as Angela answered. "No. We're not bound by vows of celibacy, though I've read about those kinds of religious communities in the histories. As a healer-in-training I'm bound only by the ancient Oath of Hippocrates."

Relief zinging through him, Zeke waited a moment more, then tentatively tried for a sitting position. Surprise filled him when his head remained clear this time.

"So there are males in this settlement?" he asked, curious. He'd never met another human male who wasn't one of his genetically engineered brothers.

"Yes, of course," Agatha replied.

"Amazing." Zeke knew he'd have to get word back to Command about these people. To his knowledge there were no other uninfected colonies anywhere.

His angel took a seat beside him, her cute little

butt resting on the bed near his hip as she faced him. He thought he saw admiration in her eyes as she looked at his bare chest a moment before she shuttered her gaze.

"How do you feel now?" Her voice was low as she busied herself with the items on the tray she'd brought.

"Better, thank you." How he wished she'd look up at him, but he had to get his mind off her and onto business. There was a reason he crash-landed on this rock, and it had to come first. "Did any of your people have a chance to look at my ship?"

That got her gaze back to his. "Ship?"

"I suppose that answers my question." He pulled the covers down, ignoring the fact that he was naked, and examined his leg. It looked sound enough, but standing would be the real test. He shifted himself to the side of the bed and stood.

* * * *

Angela held her breath, shocked at his behavior. A look from her sent Agatha scrambling from the room to get help.

"I said you could sit up, not get up." Her voice was breathless even to her own ears as she got a good look at him, naked as the day he was born, testing the support of his newly healed leg. She moved around the bed to stand in front of him should he need her help-at least, that's what she told herself she was doing. She didn't really want a better look at the marvelous male flesh revealed so enticingly before her. Did she?

Angela had seen naked men a few times before in her role as healer, but the men of the colony didn't look like this! This male was totally out of her experience. Ruggedly handsome and muscled in a way that made her mouth water, this male was like those in the storycubes from beforetimes. He was magnificent.

"It feels good as new." He put his weight on the leg that had been broken and smiled at her. There was a twinkle in his eye she had never seen before in any male. It appealed to her on some basic level with which she was altogether unfamiliar. "Thank you, sweetheart."

He leaned in, impossibly closer, until his warm lips settled over hers. Her eyebrows went up in alarm as he pulled her in with his big hands until her open palms rested against his warm, naked chest, his hardening cock poking against her thighs through the thin fabric of her dress.

He was becoming aroused! And he was kissing her like she'd never been kissed before. It felt like he put his soul into it, his tongue seeking entrance to her mouth and slipping in as she gasped. The gasp was from the action of his mobile hands, one cupping her ass and pressing her firmly against his erection, the other slipping between them to pinch one nipple hard enough to make her moan.

"Little Angel, do you feel what you do to me?" His lips nibbled down her jaw, lingering at her ear and biting down on the lobe just enough to make her squeak. Then he buried his mouth in her neck, his tongue laving her skin as if she were a sweet treat.

Now both of his hands kneaded her ass, pulling

her into his hardness with a rhythm she followed almost helplessly. He felt so good!

* * * *

"Are all the Sons of Amber as randy as you, Ezekiel?"

The woman's commanding voice came from the doorway, breaking through the sensual spell. Zeke pulled back but he could not let go of the petite bundle in his arms. He merely looked to the door where the Mother of this little enclave waited, an indulgent and slightly amused expression on her lovely features.

"Yes, ma'am." He winked. "Especially when in such lovely company."

His little angel blushed, delighting him. He felt so drawn to this one lovely little woman it amazed him. Never before had he felt such an immediate, soul-deep attraction for a particular female, and he had bedded thousands since he was grown enough to do so. First he'd been clinically taught how to pleasure a woman by the female doctors and scientists in Dr. Amber Waithe's facility. His performance had been graded, his semen collected and tested repeatedly for viability. He'd had no real youth. Accelerated growth in the incubators meant he had come to consciousness in early adolescence, just as his reproductive organs stirred to life.

Dr. Amber had overseen his progress, along with her team. They were all female and each of them had taught him and his brothers a thing or two about how to please a woman, in their own way. By the time he was ready for his duties outside the lab, he had fucked most of the women there for training purposes and some just because they wanted a male between their thighs. Sex was never in short supply for him, either at the lab or since he'd left there to assume his duties with the defense forces.

It was part of his duty to bed willing females, as well as producing sperm deposits at regular intervals so females from many different human planets and colonies could be impregnated with his or any of his brother's sperm whenever they wished. He didn't know exactly how many children he had fathered by now, but Amber and her scientists kept meticulous track. He knew there were probably hundreds, if not thousands, of little boys running around the various human worlds with his DNA by now, and the thought gave him solace.

Something of him would live on to help humanity survive. At least in this way, his life up to this point had some meaning. Still, in the dark of night, something about his life bothered him, leaving him unfulfilled. He had come to realize that something was missing, but he wasn't exactly sure what it was. The old storycubes he'd seen from beforetimes showed a much different existence than the one he was living now, where one man and one woman would live their lives together in partnership, and love.

He'd never felt love, and it was something he wanted to experience at least once before his Risker's nature led to one risk too many. He looked down at the gentle creature still held tightly in his embrace and realized that if he could experience love, he would want to try it with someone exactly like this little angel. Perhaps he could make her love him, though he hadn't a clue how to go about it.

"Why are you looking at me like that?" his angel whispered, her dewy eyes staring up at him.

"You are the most beautiful thing I have ever beheld."

Her eyes melted and her lips softened with desire. He would have claimed yet another kiss from her at that moment, but the Mother cleared her throat rather loudly, reminding them both of her presence. How could he have forgotten she was there?

Zeke turned to face the woman in the doorway, keeping Angela in his arms. He shifted so she stood slightly in front of him, both facing the woman by the door. His hard length pressed between the cheeks of her ass, with only the thin barrier of her dress between them, as if it had found its home.

"Mother Rachel, I-" Angela didn't struggle in his arms, which he found intensely gratifying for some reason. He could tell by the rising flush on the delicate skin of her neck and the heat of her cheek against his hand that she was embarrassed.

The older woman held up her hand to forestall his angel's words, a benevolent smile on her serene features. She advanced into the room and took a seat in the chair at his bedside, inviting them to sit with a wave of her fingers. Zeke levered himself down on the bed to sit, keeping Angela in his arms. She was such a little thing it was easy to maneuver her about, like a little doll. He kept her in his lap, turning her cheek into his chest as he leaned back against the headboard of the small bed, facing the other woman.

"Ezekiel, I have the gift of foresight. It's that gift which has helped me lead this colony for many years. Most of our people have gifts of one kind or another, but the one in each generation with the strongest foresight is chosen as leader." She bowed her head modestly, but her knowing eyes did not leave his. "I have foreseen the danger you bring to our people-and the hope of salvation for all humanity. Your actions in the next few days will bring either disaster or epiphany."

Zeke shook his head, barely able to believe what this woman claimed. Sure, paranormal abilities had been documented among humans from time to time, but it was a rare thing indeed. For certain, he'd never met anyone who claimed to be able to see the future before.

The woman smiled and he saw a light of challenge in her eyes. "You crashed here on the run from jit pirates, is that not so?"

"Well, yeah." Zeke was amazed by her knowledge, but then it could be she'd arrived at the conclusion through a process of deduction. Or maybe a lucky guess.

"They search for you. Within three cycles, they will find your crash site. You must get there first."

Zeke felt the back of his neck itch. "I'd planned to go out as soon as it got dark. There are some things on my ship I could use and I have to try to contact my base."

The Mother nodded. "Good. It will be dark soon." She checked her chronometer. "Sister Angela will accompany you."

"Begging your pardon, ma'am, but I work better

alone." He felt the little woman in his arms stiffen. "Sweetheart, you'd only slow me down. I'll be back before you know it."

The Mother stood. "No. You don't understand. There are creatures that hunt in the darkness on this planet. You don't know their ways. Sister Angela goes with you to protect you."

He couldn't help it. He laughed out loud at the idea the little woman in his arms would need to defend him from any sort of predator. She struggled to leave his embrace, but he wouldn't allow it.

"Whoa, there. I'm sorry, angel, but I'm a trained warrior. I'm not used to the idea of a woman protecting me. It's usually the other way around."

"Not here," the Mother said with finality in her tone. "You'll soon learn why, so don't question what you don't yet understand. We've lived here for a long time. We know this planet and its creatures."

Zeke could see the wisdom in that and backed down as graciously as possible. Besides, having his angel nearby made him feel good in a way he didn't quite understand.

Chapter Two

An hour later, Zeke found himself in a rattletrap of a land vehicle, chugging along the darkening surface of the most inhospitable ball of rock he'd ever seen. If not for the hidden settlement below ground, there was no way human life could last for long on the hard-baked surface. The all-too-close binary suns saw to that.

He heard a strange barking call off to his left at the same time he noticed Angela scrambling to add some kind of cone-shaped device to the gunnery position in the rear of the vehicle. She'd given him a basic course in driving the thing, then taken up a vigilant stance behind the gunmount after they left the series of tunnels and emerged onto the surface.

"What is that?" He sped the little craft along, homing in on his crash site using the small handcomp that had been in the pocket of his flight suit. It was a minor miracle the somewhat delicate handcomp had come through the crash and Zeke's ordeal on the baking surface of the planet without a scratch. Good thing the short-range locator beacon on the ship was still functional, too. He knew he could at least find the ship, but what condition it would be in when he got there, he had no idea.

Zeke was in a lot of pain when he left the ship

BIANCA D'ARC

days before and not focused on its post-crash condition. Instead he was more concerned with finding shelter from the binary suns and a little delirious with pain from a nasty head injury. He couldn't recall exactly what had been damaged on his ship. He knew it was in reasonable shape, but also that it wouldn't be flying anytime soon.

"*Gaks*." Angela spit the word at him and he took a moment to look back at her disgusted face.

"What?"

"*Gaks*. They hunt in packs. Depending on the size of the pack that's tracking us, we can probably handle them. They have huge ears and hunt by sound. That's what this is for." She pointed to the conical device now on the end of her energy cannon. "It's a wave amplifier. I can chase quite a few of them away with one well-placed shot, but they come at you from all directions. How we do will depend on how many there are following us."

He listened to the sounds of the desert night, understanding almost immediately why the colonists had named the creatures *gaks*. It was the sound of their cries. Like short coughs, multiplied over and over, the creatures called out to each other with that eerie noise. Judging by the number of calls, there were at least fifteen to twenty of the things coming up on either side of them, but luckily, they were nearing the ship.

If he could get them to it quickly enough, maybe he could use what remained of the shielding to keep the *gaks* at bay. Nothing on the surface of any planet could get through the energy shielding on his ship. It was designed to keep interstellar debris from fouling his engines down to the level of cosmic dust. It would surely keep out a bunch of odd sounding pack animals.

Without warning, Angela fired the cannon mounted atop the rickety land vehicle. The whole thing shuddered. Zeke turned his head in time to see three of the most hideously ugly creatures he'd ever seen scrambling away. They had long, pointed ears and big snouts filled with sharp teeth. They were an indeterminate gray color and ran nimbly on four legs, using an additional two front appendages like short arms.

Angela fired again and five more went running from his right.

"Keep driving!" she called, aiming and firing again. More creatures ran, but even more came rushing in to take their place.

He pushed the little rattletrap vehicle as fast as it would go. They were almost there.

Angela was firing continuously now, but the creatures kept coming. Zeke tried to devise a plan to get them inside the ship and hopefully to safety, but he wasn't sure if the ship was whole enough to keep the *gaks* out. It was a risk, but then, he was a Risker. This was the kind of thing he'd been born to do.

Tapping out a series of commands on his handcomp, he prayed to the Maker that the bay doors were still functional. When he saw a growing light in the distance he released the breath he'd been holding. The bay ramp was lowering and the light from within the cargo hold shone brightly as it was revealed. Now if he could time this just right, he could get himself, Angela, and this crazy little land vehicle inside, the bay door shut again, and the shield up before the *gaks* found a way in through any of the wrecked areas of the ship.

* * * *

Zeke's risky plan worked like a charm. Only a few of the *gaks* tried to follow them up the ramp but Angela repelled them with a final blast from the energy cannon. The rise of the bay door prevented any of the other creatures from entering that way.

Zeke vaulted from the land vehicle and headed for the computer console as soon as he was inside. He felt Angela following at a slower pace.

"Thank the Maker." Zeke input his codes and raised the ship's shield. It was intact and more than powerful enough to repel the night creatures. He turned to look down at his little angel, standing quietly at his side. "We're safe for the moment. The *gaks* can't breach the shield."

Adrenaline pumping through him, he couldn't help but reach for her. She came willingly into his arms and raised her lips to his. The feel of her made his senses swim, the taste of her fired his blood, but he knew there was something he had to do first, before he gave in to the temptation of her lush, young body. Straining against his desire, he set her away from him.

"We have work to do, before pleasure." He couldn't resist swooping in to place a silly kiss on the tip of her nose. "I assume the *gaks* will scurry away just before the suns rise?"

She nodded. "All the hunters and prey retreat in

the hour before dawn."

"Good." He turned back to the console and tapped a few more commands. "Until then, I have to check the status of my ship and communications gear. I need to try to get a message to my base." He looked over the readouts to be certain the shield would hold. He could also access internal diagnostics from this station to make certain nothing indigenous to the planet had already found its way into the ship to lie in wait for them.

"Everything looks clean. At least I remembered to seal the hatch before I took off across the surface in search of help." He laughed at himself and the damage a little bump on the head could do to an otherwise sane individual. "I don't know what I was thinking." He paused a moment, facing away from Angela, but he could almost feel her curious eyes boring into his back. "At the time, I could've sworn I heard someone, or maybe something, calling out to me."

He turned to face her as she shrugged. It was not the reaction he expected.

"Why aren't you surprised?"

"Maybe you did hear something. Such things happen among our people. It's not that astonishing to think a higher power would help you find your way to us." Her eyes evaded him as she went on, her cheeks flushing just the tiniest bit. "I normally don't make a habit of roaming the surface in the middle of the day either, but I knew I had to go out that day. Perhaps you were calling to us as much as we called to you."

"Fate?" he mused, reaching out to slip a finger

under her chin, raising her eyes to meet his once more. "You think it was meant to be that you found me and saved my life?"

She nodded slightly. "So the Mother said. How else can you explain it?"

He let her go and shook his head, starting for the inner bay doors. "I can't." He waited for her to join him before heading out into the corridor that led to the command center of his mid-sized ship. He'd have to do the rest of his checks from there, and if the comm systems were working, that's also where he'd find them.

* * * *

An hour later, Zeke threw the wrench he'd been using to the floor in disgust.

"There's no way to conceal a transmission. The scrambler's dead."

"What does that mean?" Angela came up beside him, her warm presence reminding him of the reason for his haste.

"If I send out an unscrambled transmission, the jit pirates will be able to see exactly what I'm sending. Even worse, the scrambling unit also holds the camouflage circuits. If I send out a broadband signal without them engaged, there's no way to hide its point of origin, so the jits will know exactly where we are in addition to what we're saying." Frustration ate at him.

"That's not good."

"You're good at understatement, aren't you?" He looked up into her eyes, finding humor there, and

27

immediately his tense shoulders relaxed. There was something so comforting about her mere presence, even when the comm system was shot to hell and back. All she had to do was smile at him and everything was suddenly okay. Even if it wasn't.

"Is there a way to narrow your transmission? To aim it so that only your people receive it?"

Zeke sat back, thinking for a moment. "You just might have something there. It's old tech. Narrow beam hasn't been used in years since it requires precise calculations and maps, but I was on a mapping mission as I approached your planet, so I have the most up-to-date data available. If the mapper isn't fried as well." He stood, taking a quick moment to cup her shoulders and deliver a smacking kiss to her lips before putting her aside so he could get to a different console in the tight command area.

He felt her watching over his shoulder as he tapped some commands into the state of the art mapping unit. She jumped when the holo display zipped to life, its gentle glow lighting the cabin as he brought up a three dimensional representation of his route from the base on Atlantia Prime to his current position.

"Is that where you came from?" Her voice brushed past his ear, reminding him how he wanted this dark night to end-if he could just get his transmission sent. With the jit threat looming, duty had to come first.

"Yes. Atlantia Station is headquarters for the Quadrant Regimental Command. If I get this right, I might be able to tight beam directly to them." He tapped out a few more calculations, feeding coordinates into two consoles now, utilizing both hands.

* * * *

"How do you do that?" Angela was amazed by the way he could perform two tasks at once, as if both of his hands operated independently of the other.

"Sweetheart, I was genetically engineered by one of the most brilliant minds in human history. All the Sons of Amber were designed to be multi-taskers with above average intellectual abilities. It's no big deal." He looked up at her and shrugged, his hands continuing their work all the while he talked to her, further astonishing her.

"Amazing."

"Hold on, I think we're about ready to try this." He winked at her and put all his attention on the comm console, leaning in to the vid pickup. "There's some risk involved in this," he took a moment to meet her eyes, pausing before he input the final commands, "but I believe it will work."

"Mother Rachel believes it's our only chance. Without help from your people, the jits will find us anyway. If your signal goes astray, it will only speed up the inevitable."

He touched her hand with his, squeezing softly. "Have a little faith. I may be a Risk Taker, but I never take foolish risks."

"I trust you, Ezekiel."

"Call me Zeke, Angel." He squeezed her hand once more and turned back to touch the final sequence on the console. After a few flickers, the screen came to life.

"Atlantia Station, this is Ezekiel Amber. Mayday. Mayday. Mayday. Come in Atlantia Station. Over." He sat back and reached for her hand, pulling her down on his lap. "It will take some time for the signal to reach them and a few moments for any return signal. I'm keeping the beam open so they'll know to piggyback on it and not blow my location. It's standard operating procedure when comming with someone in my position."

"For a spy, you mean?" His muscles twitched slightly under her and she realized with some satisfaction that she'd managed to surprise him. "Well, isn't that what you are? Why else would you be roaming out here alone, mapping empty space?"

He kissed her nose. "You're a pretty smart lady, but the proper term for what I was doing is reconnaissance. I was gathering intelligence on the buildup of jit pirates in this sector and ran smack into the middle of them."

"Not such a good spy, then, are you?" She teased him, and he retaliated with a kiss. His lips devoured hers, his tongue tangling with hers so deliciously they almost missed the crackle and hiss of the comm system as the response came in. She could see the excitement in his eyes as his gamble paid off. He had such beautiful eyes.

"Zeke! Where the hell are you, brother? I've mobilized half the fleet looking for you. Over."

She pulled back, surprised by the handsome man's image on the comm screen. He looked a lot like Ezekiel in build and the sharpness of his attractive facial features, but his hair was dark as midnight, where Zeke's was a lighter shade of honey brown. His eyes however, were harder, harsher, and darker, almost as if they had seen too much of the worst of life.

Ezekiel didn't seem to mind that she was on his lap as he answered, though she was clearly in view of the vid pickup.

"Michael! I'm glad you're there. I got hit by jit pirates and crash-landed on a planet with binary suns. There are people here, Mike. An uncontaminated colony of humans. I repeat: uncontaminated. The jits are coming back for me and I need your help, buddy, before they find me and bring the virus to these good folk. I'm sending the coordinates layered under the vid on this message, plus any other data that survived the crash. I hope your techs can make some use of it. Over."

He sat back again, taking her mouth with aggressive joy that she felt down to her toes. "We did it!" He came up for air long enough to beam at her. "Mike will send help. I'm betting some of our ships are already in the sector, looking for me. We'll be able to defend your people against the jits."

He kissed her again and again, sending her senses swimming as her passion awakened. The man knew how to kiss! And his hands weren't still, either. Those talented fingers of his were multi-tasking their way through her buttons and up under her skirt until one rested between her legs and the other inside her bodice, cupping her bare breast as he lightly pinched the nipple.

She squeaked at the unexpected pleasure of his

touch, but then the comm system crackled to life again and he sat back to listen.

"I'm sending *Regent*, *Regulus*, and *Reliant* to you directly. They'll secure orbit around the planet and keep the jits away. Zeke, Dr. Waithe is here and she wants you to hang tight. She's readying the *Sultana* as we speak and they'll be heading for you. She wants to examine the colony, if they're agreeable. The first of the battleships should arrive within five standards. Dr. Waithe will arrive on board *Sultana* in twenty. In the meantime, you are to protect the colonists at all costs. I don't need to tell you how important they could be to the survival of humanity." Angela watched the harsh man's serious eyes turn amused as he winked. "And judging by the pretty little girl on your lap, you won't mind this duty at all. Over."

"You got that right. I can't complain at all." Zeke squeezed her waist with the hand he had thankfully removed from her bodice. She was covered, but just barely. "This is my angel of mercy, Sister Angela. She saved my life after the crash and healed my broken bones. The colony here, from what little I've been able to observe, is about fifty percent male, Mike. Regular, normal, healthy human males, like from the beforetimes. I never thought I'd see such a thing. They're led by a woman who claims to have the ability to see the future and she believes the jits will find us sooner rather than later, so we'll definitely need the firepower those three battleships can provide. My ship is badly damaged and no longer space worthy. The scrambler's toast, hence the odd manner of transmitting this message."

He raised his eyebrows as he looked around the command cabin. "According to my calculations, we'll be losing the direct beam in another few minutes, so this is probably my last transmission. The jit pirates patrol this sector in force. Hopefully you'll be able to pull my logs off the sub-channel I've been streaming. I have a working handcomp and not much else. Please tell the captains to comm me directly when they reach orbit on my registered access number." He paused, and Angela could see the relief in his eyes. "And thanks, Mike. I owe you one, brother. Big time. Over."

He sat back and ran one hand through his hair in relief. Angela moved to cup his stubbly cheek in her hand, rubbing gently. He felt so good.

"Now, where were we?"

His eyes danced as he moved the chair back, hitting a lever that turned the command chair into a couch-like surface that many solo pilots used for sleeping on long hauls without leaving the command cabin.

Ezekiel's lips latched onto hers as his hands lifted her dress up and off, exposing her skin to lightly moving air in the ventilated cabin. It felt good, brushing delicately over her skin, but his hands felt even better.

He held her over him, her breasts dangling over his mouth as he raised her. With a playful snarl, he nipped at her heavy breasts, catching the nipples between his lips. He drew lightly on the tips, then harder as she began to shiver with excitement. He spent some time playing with her breasts while she squirmed over him, straddling his lean hips, placing her knees on either side as her dress bunched around her waist and hips.

His hands moved lower to pull up her dress. He pushed aside her panties and squeezed the globes of her ass in both hands while he continued to suck on her nipples in turn. Tugging her down, he pressed his engorged cock up into her folds, only the material of his pants between them now.

"We've lifted your data from the beam and I'm looking through it now," Michael's voice came back over the comm. She looked back to see the man's face on the vid pickup, glad the vid was in receive mode rather than send mode as Zeke let go of her and raised up on his elbows so he could see the last of his brother's message.

"The battleship *Regulus* should reach you first. They're closest. We'll upload your data to the other battleships as well. Holy shit, Zeke." Mike's face on the vid screen showed him reading a smaller screen at his side. She guessed that one was probably scrolling the data Zeke had transmitted. "I knew you Riskers were all a little crazy, but you ran into a lot more than you bargained for if what I'm seeing in your data stream about the enemy force is accurate. I'm amazed you made it, but then you've always led a charmed life." On the screen, Michael looked up and smiled. He has a beautiful smile, she thought absently, one that invited a woman closer, though his chiseled features laid down the law about who would be in charge.

"I'm authorizing full deployment on this. If you really have found yourself a colony of uninfected humans, their protection will be our highest priority.

Please reassure them of that and lay some groundwork for us. If that pretty girl on your lap is any indication, they seem to like you." The dark man chuckled wryly. "We'll be there as soon as possible. Hold on 'til then, brother, and be well. I won't expect a reply. We see your charts and the planet you're on will be occluded shortly. Stay safe. Over."

Chapter Three

Zeke watched the transmission sputter out as the heavens shifted and the beam was lost. He turned back to the warm, willing woman on his lap. At least, he hoped he was reading her right and she was as willing as he to explore the passion between them. He tightened his arms around her as his eyes met hers.

"Do you want this, my angel? Will you let me make love to you?"

He paused, holding his breath. Never before had a woman's answer to that question meant so much to him. His angel was special in every way. He wanted her and wanted to please her in return. While he always made it a point to give satisfaction to his bed partners, his angel deserved so much more. He would give her everything he was, ecstasy beyond anything she had ever known before, and he knew somehow he would achieve the same-but only in the arms of this small woman, his angel.

Angela surprised him by pushing his chest back until he was reclining on the pilot's couch. She moved down until her warm breath was pulsing softly over the bulge at his crotch. Zeke groaned as her hands traced the length of him under his pants.

"The question should be, will you let me

pleasure you, Son of Amber?"

Her soft voice was temptation itself.

"When you ask so nicely, how could I refuse?"

His eyes danced as he grinned at her, but soft moans came from his throat a moment later when Angela used her delicate little hands to unfasten his pants and release his straining member. She laughed as his hard cock popped free of the confining material and sought her attention. A moment later, she licked him, stroking him with her tongue. Her shy, yet bold touch affected him like nothing else in the universe.

She took him down deep and hollowed out her cheeks, sucking hard, her talented little tongue darting around his sensitive shaft. He groaned as she stroked him, her hands fingering his balls with gentle caresses. He looked down and found her gorgeous eyes looking back at him, her mouth tight around his length. Something inside him broke free and took flight.

That look. If he could just keep that happy, sexy look on her face forever, he would die a happy man. She felt so right in his arms, so precious, not to mention precocious as she played with his body. He felt her delight in the curve of her lips, the soft stroke of her fingers and the sparkling light in her eyes. How he adored her!

Many women had used their mouths on him in prelude to fucking, but Angela seemed to just want to suck and suck him. Never mind her pleasure, her focus seemed to be totally on his enjoyment. That wasn't quite what he wanted, but he was too weak to pull back. He wanted her in every possible way. He wanted her surrender, her care, her intimate attention. Why? He wasn't sure. But he wasn't up to questioning the driving instincts inside him.

"Ease up, honey. I'm coming." He tried to pull away, to spare her the force of the eruption he could feel building, but she stayed firm, her gaze challenging him saucily.

In a blinding rush, he came in her mouth, spurting long and hard. She swallowed repeatedly, but still some of his thick cum trickled out the sides of her mouth, so much did he give her. Looking down into her sparkling eyes, his heart lifted as she smiled back at him, licking and swallowing as she cleaned him thoroughly like a well-satisfied kitten.

"You like that?" He couldn't help the teasing tone in his voice or the smile that lit his lips. This small woman was so special to him. No woman of his experience had ever given him so much or so freely.

She moaned her agreement, licking the tip of him that still leaked the last of his cum.

"I like the taste of you, Ezekiel. Salty and sweet at the same time."

He could tell her that the Sons of Amber had been created to have pleasant tasting body fluids, but this moment was more than just well designed parts fitting into place. This moment was magic, if a practical man like him believed in such things. He dragged her up for a kiss, loving the taste of his cum on her lips, like it belonged there.

When he drew back, he laved licking kisses all down her throat to her breasts, sucking them lightly, playing with the tips until he felt her shiver.

"Now it's your turn."

She pulled back with a question in her eyes. "Don't you need a moment to recover?"

Zeke laughed as he switched their positions, moving her easily beneath him on the couch. When he was sure she was settled comfortably, he knelt , positioning himself between her thighs as he arranged them to his liking-spread wide apart on either side of his hips. As it should be.

He noticed when she looked down and gave a little start of surprise. His dick was hard again, ready, willing, and able. He couldn't help but grin as his gaze roved up the length of her luscious body, finally meeting her lovely eyes as he moved over her.

"One of the benefits of being genetically designed to repopulate the human race is that unlike most males, I don't need much downtime. I'm always ready. Especially for you, sweetheart." He leaned down and kissed her sweetly, meaning every word and every lick of his adoring tongue.

"Oh, my!" She gasped as he raised his lips just slightly, holding her gaze as he found his way inside her for the first time. She was slick and warm-more than ready for him.

He slid within her tight hole, going slowly so as not to hurt her. It was torture of the sweetest kind. She was wet and excited, but he could tell from the tight confines of her pussy that she hadn't done this in a while.

"Tell me if you're uncomfortable, Angel. I don't want to hurt you."

She held his gaze as he moved in further. "No. I'm okay." She was panting now, and it was music to his ears. "It's just that I've only done this once before."

He moved slightly, working his way inside her until he was settled, all the way home in her core. He stilled and looked deep into her eyes. He was glad that this meant something to her, that this was more than just a casual fuck. He knew it meant more than that to him. Never before in his life had anything felt remotely like this. This mattered. It touched his heart to know she might feel the same.

"I'm honored beyond words."

She blushed so prettily, he had to kiss her. Then as he kissed her, he decided he had to move within her. The hot center of her was heaven itself and oh, so tempting. Slowly at first, he began to rock in and out of her, watching her face and keeping his senses open to her responses. She was so precious, so perfect, so trusting of what he was doing and so open to the experience. He could hardly ask for anything more in a partner. He was fast realizing that she was his ideal woman.

Increasing his pace, he laid claim to her fully, his thrusts harder and more powerful. Her hands roved over his back, the short nails digging in when he went deep, searching for that magic spot he knew would send her into orbit.

"There?" he asked as her nails raked him yet again, the finest of tortures.

"Yes!" She nodded against his chest as he grinned and stayed deep within, rocking slowly to rub her sweet spot. "Yes, Ezekiel. Yes!"

He felt a profound satisfaction within him as her tight sheath spasmed around him. She climaxed hard, but it was only the first of many he would give her. He let her come down only a little before stroking deep and fast once more. Increasing his thrusts and his rhythm, he changed position slightly until he heard her gasp in pleasure.

"Ready for more, Angel?"

"Ezekiel!"

After that it took little to bring her to peak after peak. Zeke smiled all through the waves of her pleasure, feeling his own passion multiplied by her obvious enjoyment of his attentions. He thrust faster and harder, following the sway of her hips as she shattered in a frenzy around him yet again.

Eventually, Zeke let go, bathing her womb in his cum, planting his seed firmly within the woman he prized above all others. She came again as his hot cum shot into her, setting off waves of orgasm that took them both on a wild ride.

When Zeke could think again, he levered himself upwards, unwilling to leave her body. He kept himself planted within her, supporting her with his arms as he stood from the couch, carrying her slowly toward the hatch that led to the main corridor of the ship. His dick lengthened once more as Angela's eyes shot open. He could read the flames of passion there, banked but coming back to life even as he moved them both slowly along the corridor toward his private chamber.

He got her to the wide bed before they both climaxed again, then they dozed for a bit, wrapped in each other's arms. Waking later, they made love again and again until neither had the energy to resist sleep's call. Zeke set the alarm to wake him two hours before sunrise. He still had work to do on the ship, but it would have to wait until later. For now, he had to take care of his woman.

* * * *

Several hours later, Angela woke, disoriented at first until she felt the hard, male arms wrapped tightly around her waist.

Ezekiel.

She savored his name in her mind as his arms tightened on her bare body. He slept still, but his strong yet tender hold never slackened. Even lost in the netherwold of sleep, he kept her close.

It had to mean something, but she feared she might be putting too much stock in dreams. She wanted this man from the stars with a passion unknown to her before. Since she'd found him under the burning midday suns, her life had changed in irreversible ways. Her heart had come alive and her body pulsated with yearnings she didn't fully understand, but knew he had the cure.

The cure for her woeful condition was him. His love, his passion, his cum filling her body. She wanted it all. Especially his heart.

But there were so many obstacles, not the least of which was the role he had been designed and bred to perform. If she understood him correctly, he was some kind of intergalactic super stud, sent out among the remnants of humanity to service any and all females who wanted his sperm. In one way, the thought disgusted her, but in another more perverse part of her psyche, the thought was tantalizing. To think that she held him-this man whom so many women desired-and he was with her. Not normally given to vanity, the feeling of pride sat uncomfortably in her mind, as did the jealousy.

Angela felt like scratching the eyes out of any woman who'd had him before. She wanted to mark him, to stake her claim and let all other females know that while they might bear his children, they would never have his heart. His heart was hers alone.

Or so she dreamed.

Her dreams spoke of love everlasting, but she had yet to discover whether these were prophetic dreams so common to many of her people, or, just dreams of what her inner self wished could be. She prayed the dreams would come to pass. She prayed mightily that she could keep Ezekiel in her life-and in her bed-where he belonged. Never before had she felt such a strong, deep, and instant connection in her soul for any other person, male or female.

She knew the moment she saw him, baking under the sun and close to death, that he was simply hers. Just as she was his. They were fated to be together, their hearts and souls entwined. Now she just had to see if her thoughts and hopes could truly be reality or if they were just foolish dreams.

Then there was his duty as a Son of Amber to contend with. How could she claim the sole attentions of a male so important to the survival of the entire human species? Was it fair of her to want to keep him for herself? Was it even possible? Only time would tell, and those whose in authority, who would make the decision to separate them and send him away, or let him stay and be with her.

There was also the all-important question too, of whether he would want to stay. Could she be misreading his responses? She had little experience of men, but she thought she felt possessiveness and care in his every movement against her, his every embrace. Still he had yet to say the words. Did he want her in his life on a long-term basis or was this just another pleasant interlude for him in his never-ending duties to fuck every woman he met?

She thought not, but still the uncertainty lingered.

Pushing the dreadful questions from her mind, she sighed as he woke behind her, his large body rubbing against her as he stretched.

"What are you doing awake?" His deep voice rumbled sexily in her ear, making her shiver.

Turning in his arms, she insinuated one of her legs between his, rubbing his reviving cock with her thigh. Her eyes teased him as a smile played about her lips.

"I was waiting for you to wake up, Ezekiel. I was getting lonely without you inside me. I feel so empty."

He grinned as he pulled her even more intimately against him. "That can be easily remedied, my little angel. You'll never be empty if I have anything to say about it."

With a tender shove, he filled her, rocking them both gently this time to an explosive climax. They basked in the glow for long, long moments, staring deep into each other's eyes. Angela reveled in his soft caresses as he held her close and snuggled deep in her heart and soul. It was more than just a physical thing, she would stake her life on it.

* * * *

Sometime later, they dressed and made their way back up to the cockpit. Zeke ran a few more checks while introducing Angela to the various features of his ship. She browsed around while he worked, looking at the equipment and asking a few questions here and there that he enjoyed answering. She was bright and sharp as a tack. He liked her quick wit almost as much as he loved her supple body and giving, passionate nature.

He schooled his thoughts and went back to the task at hand. He had work to do after all, and though she was a gorgeous distraction, her safety and the safety of her people depended on him. That thought in mind, he settled down to formulate his next moves.

"I think we can fly this ship closer to the entrance of your settlement."

"Is that safe?" Angela's voice echoed her hesitation.

"Well, I wouldn't trust the seals to hard vacuum, but it should be sound enough for a short atmospheric hop."

"No," she shook her head softly, setting her lovely hair to swaying, distracting him momentarily. "I mean won't the jits see your ship faster if it's out in the open near our entrance rather than among these rocks?"

"Actually, they've already pinged it twice with their mapping gear, but the camo unit is still online and sending out false readings. The jits wouldn't be able to tell if we're a ship or just another large rock formation unless they do a visual inspection. We'll see them long before that, if they head downplanet."

"How?" Her beautiful eyes scrunched up in concern. "We don't have any scanners to detect incoming ships, or we would have seen you long before I went searching after your smoke trail on the horizon."

He thought about that a moment. This young woman had set out in the middle of the blindingly bright day after an unknown smoke trail, all on her own. Her courage amazed him. She had saved his life, without a doubt. Now he would protect her and her people to the best of his ability. He'd be damned if he let the jits bring their deadly virus to these peaceful folk.

"This ship has scanners capable of alerting me to any movement within three hundred and sixty degrees. Luckily they're still working. I can rig them to signal my handcomp when I'm not aboard if something comes near enough to be a problem and I can always fire up the engines and evade if necessary. The weapons systems are also still online, so we have some offensive as well as defensive capabilities."

"Sounds like you have all the angles covered." Her smile was complimentary and it warmed him.

"Honey, it's in my nature to take risks, but I also know and examine all the probabilities before I choose a course of action. Dr. Waithe designed it that way so our risk taking tendencies wouldn't get us killed too easily. My mind works a little differently than most humans. I can calculate probabilities almost like a computer, but with the emotional component that even the best Artificial Intelligence units can't duplicate." He stood and ushered her over to a secondary co-pilot position that was tucked up into the bulkhead. He hadn't needed the extra seat, flying solo before he crashed, but it came in handy now. "Trust me when I say I've examined all our options and come up with the best available plan of action."

She seemed to consider his words carefully before she spoke. "Okay, Ezekiel." Her eyes brightened as she turned to look up at him. "I think I'd enjoy taking a little ride in your ship. I've never been in a space worthy vessel before."

He chuckled. "Well, this one isn't space worthy at the moment, but I get your meaning. We'll just hop over to the settlement and park it among the small hills that hide the entrance. I have a map of where the jits have already pinged this side of the planet since I crashed so we can set down somewhere they haven't already mapped."

"Good idea." She settled into the small seat he drew out from the bulkhead for her.

"Strap in and we'll fire up the engines."

* * * *

Angela was a little frightened at first when the ship lurched off the ground.

"Sorry for the bumpy ride. This thing isn't space worthy, but she's just fine for an atmospheric run. Don't worry."

"If you say so." She rolled her eyes and they both chuckled.

After a few minutes of smooth movement through the atmosphere, Angela began to relax. Ezekiel brought up a viewscreen so she could observe the ground from above. According to him they were just high enough to clear the tallest of the mountains, though to her that was more than enough altitude. Still, since this craft was intended to sail the vast vacuum of space, she realized this little hop up into the atmosphere was nothing to him.

"It's beautiful from up here."

She meant every word as the rugged terrain of her homeworld dazzled her senses. From this altitude the suns were already lighting a good portion of the land below in shimmering golds, browns, and reds. It was breathtaking.

"Pretty planet from this vantage point," Ezekiel agreed, "but damned inhospitable to live on. Someday, Angela, I'd like to show you the warm oceans of Pacifica or the rolling grasslands of Argentia."

She heard the yearning in his tone but she also knew those worlds he spoke of were infected with the jit virus. She couldn't go there now and probably would never be able to set foot off this adopted homeworld. Still, she could dream.

"I'd like to see Espia. That's where our people originated." She remembered the beautiful green and blue forests she'd seen only in recordings. "The history cubes I've seen of it are lovely."

He leaned back in his chair as she noticed him starting their descent sequence. "Espia is truly beautiful. The mists in the capital city burn off in the morning sun and the temperature is ideal all year round."

"You've been there?" Only the oldest of the elders now remembered their home planet and they'd been children when the colonists fled.

"Yeah, I had a stopover there last year. Spent a few weeks of downtime while my ship was serviced. It's a beautiful place, but they were hit hard by the virus. There are no males left there at all."

"None?" She gasped, thinking of all her male friends and family that would die if the virus found its way to their colony.

"Some worlds were luckier than others. A few males survived here and there on many planets, but almost all were sterile after their bout with the virus and they lived with the threat of recurrence. On a few rare worlds, the males suffered through the disease badly at first, then it went dormant, waiting to strike again at any moment." His face tightened into grim lines. "Espia was one of the few planets where all the males died in the first round of infection. Certain uniquely Espian DNA sequences and physiology made your ancestors much more susceptible to the virus than other human variants. Many of the Espian females died as well, though most females on other planets did not. Your ancestors were wise to leave." Angela sent up a silent prayer as she thought of all the dead. "The cities are pretty much empty now, with many buildings vacant. There are few people to live in the leftover spaces, but the survivors are resilient. They've learned to value what they have left of their world. Music and the arts flourish still, and new schools to study medicine and science have been opened. The few young born since the virus are encouraged to study hard and help rebuild their society."

"They're still having children then?"

"With Dr. Waithe's help." He turned away to focus on the landing as they approached the hills where the entrance to the settlement was hidden. "Sons of Amber were dispatched to the hardest hit planets as soon as we were able to perform our duties."

"Your duties?" She had a sneaking suspicion what they might entail.

He took a moment to settle the ship before answering. Once the ship was powering down, he turned to her.

"I told you when I first woke, Angel. I and my brothers were designed to help repopulate human worlds. We breed true and have certain skills and qualities that are helpful to societies starting to rebuild. Some of my brothers were dispatched to Espia to help protect them from jit raiders. Some were sent to help the scientists set up sperm banks and a breeding program. Whatever the assignment, we are always encouraged to have sex with any female that desires it."

Angela's heart plummeted. His voice sounded so clinical, so cold as he explained his bizarre 'duties.' The warmth they'd shared only hours before seeped away from her, leaving her chilled inside.

"So am I just a part of your duty, then?" She couldn't even look at him.

His warm hand tucked under her chin, raising her eyes to his. He'd moved out of his pilot's chair and to her side without making a sound.

50

"No." His eyes narrowed with some indefinable emotion. "You're different, Angela. From the moment I first saw you, everything about you has been completely out of my experience." He leaned in to kiss her softly, then pulled back. "And I admit I've had a lot of experience with women of every sort." He grinned, though she didn't like to hear that she was only one in a long line of conquests for him. "I don't know what it is about you, but when I look at you, I could care less about my duty, my mission, or anything else. All that matters is you."

His whispered words were so touching, so heartfelt, tears gathered behind her eyes.

Chapter Four

The captain of the *Regulus* commed him a little more than four standards later. He knew the captain, an older woman named Litus, having worked with her before. Gifted with a steady nerve and strong leadership skills, she'd put on all available power to get her ship to the planet even sooner than the original estimate. Since the entire planet was in quarantine until the scientists could determine whether the population was truly free of contamination by the jit virus, Captain Litus informed him the battleship was taking up a defensive position in orbit. The *Regulus* would circle with the small planet until they were joined by two other ships of the line. The three of them would then defend the colony against all comers, keeping anyone who was not duly authorized from traveling to the surface.

No way would they let anyone who had the potential of carrying the jit virus to these uninfected humans anywhere near the surface. Sons of Amber were naturally immune and had been designed so that they would never carry the virus. Scrubbers onboard all spacecraft would ensure any remnants of the virus that might be carried on inanimate objects were eradicated as soon as all hatches were shut and the air started cycling. Zeke knew his ship had been one hundred percent clean before he crashed, and it was impossible for him or any Son to carry the virus. Regular humans, though, that was another matter.

Any visitor to the colony who was not a Son would have to wear full protective gear with his own independent air supply. The risk involved in such a visit was high and Zeke knew it would not be undertaken lightly. Dr. Amber would certainly come, if she thought it was important enough, but she would take all possible precautions to prevent contamination of an uninfected human population-the first they had ever found.

Ezekiel reported all this to Mother Rachel, as leader of the colony, answering her questions about the newly arriving ships' capabilities and their crews. She seemed interested to know that each ship had a crew made up almost entirely of women, and Zeke found himself explaining how the few male survivors of the virus on each world most often stayed near their home planets at the request of the medical community. Established gender roles had changed somewhat since the devastating virus attack, and perhaps because Zeke had never known any other way of living, he was equally interested in the more traditional way the colonists divided the workload.

The men of the colony saw mostly to its defense, though occasionally a female would stand sentry duty or train in the hand-to-hand self defense style they favored. It all depended on individual interests. In this settlement, the males and females alike had the luxury of choosing to follow their own paths rather than have their roles dictated by the desperate needs of society. Watching them, Zeke realized he'd never really had any choice in what he would do with his life. He wasn't complaining. He liked what he did, but it was just a little disconcerting to realize that his choices had been sorely limited by the jits and their despicable virus.

Still, many of the Sons of Amber were involved in the military, both because it was in their natures and because of the necessity that they travel quite frequently to the other human planets. Some served in combat posts, some in planning, reconnaissance and strategy, each according to his own specific talents. None were given special treatment, but most of them excelled because it was simply the way they'd been designed. None of the Sons of Amber were mediocre, and all had a drive to succeed in their chosen fields.

Zeke's brother Michael, for example, was the commander of Atlantia Base, not because he'd been given the job, but because he'd earned it. He commanded all the ships in the sector and did a damned fine job of it. He had a quick, decisive mind, and as a Dominant it was in his nature to command any given situation.

"Tell me about your mother, Ezekiel." Mother Rachel startled him with her phrasing, but Zeke smiled.

"Dr. Amber isn't really my mother in the biological sense, ma'am, but she created the program the produced myself and the other Sons. She oversaw our development at every stage and contributed greatly to our make-up."

"She may not be your biological mother, Ezekiel," Rachel favored him with a serene smile, "but yet you love her as a son."

Zeke felt only a little uncomfortable talking about such intimate feelings with this foreign woman. It was surprising, actually, since he'd never discussed his innermost emotions with anyone before. He shrugged off the odd feeling that Mother Rachel's wise eyes held far more knowledge than she should rightly have.

"I guess all the Sons love her in one way or another. She's..." he hesitated slightly, trying to put his feelings into words. "She's a very special woman. She encourages us. She taught us from when we were just born. She gives us pep talks when we need them and hope to go on. She has a real, potent vision of the future."

Rachel's eyes glistened with approval. "Then she is your mother in all the ways that matter most. And Ezekiel," she placed one small hand on his arm, squeezing slightly to emphasize her words, "her vision will succeed. Never doubt that."

Mother Rachel went on to ask about the other people who were coming, but asked nothing of what might happen next. After her telling comments of moments before, he suspected she knew more about what might occur after his people arrived than even he did.

He spent a few minutes showing the sentries as well as some of the youngsters-a mixed group of young boys and girls-how to operate the small shield generator he'd brought out of his ship and set up at the entrance to the underground compound. With this small, portable shield spanning the entrance, the guards would be able to relax a bit and wouldn't have to face the daily skirmishes with packs of *gaks* and worse that tried constantly to get into the human dwelling areas.

The children were bright, and Zeke enjoyed their questions. He had never been around young humans much at all, and found himself enchanted by the little ones with such open, growing minds. The male sentries were hardened, fighting men, and they reminded him of the camaraderie he had only known to this point with his brothers. The only males he had ever really been exposed to were his fellow Sons. The opportunity to talk with unenhanced male humans was a rarity.

Eventually he made his way to the chamber Angela had shown him earlier, when they'd come in from his ship. It was her personal chamber. He had seen to all the tasks that needed doing, now he needed another taste of his angel's lips before he went crazy.

He knocked on the door and his insides lit when she answered with an intimate smile. She stepped back, allowing him into the small room, and he wasted no time pulling her into his arms.

"I've missed you so much." He breathed the words into her ear, delighted when she shivered.

"It's only been a few hours." Her girlish giggle made his dick quiver.

"Too long. I'm a starving man."

He crowded her back toward the small bed on which she obviously slept. He examined it over her shoulder for a quick moment. It was too small for

BIANCA D'ARC

what he had in mind, but he'd make do. He pushed down on her shoulders until she was sitting before him on the edge of her little bed.

Her little hands traced the ridge of flesh that twitched under his pants.

"Is this normal? As a healer in training, I've been taught that men aren't usually this...um...potent."

Zeke shrugged. "It's normal for me. At least when it comes to you, Angel."

He would have said more, but a knock on the hatch interrupted. Angela shot up from the bed and went to answer the door, just cracking it so she could talk with whomever was on the other side. He heard soft, feminine voices, and a moment later she shut the door and returned to him.

Pulling her again into his arms, he nuzzled her ear. "Let's go out to my ship. I've got a big, comfortable bed in my cabin, and no one can intrude on us there once I put the shield up."

Her expression teased as she looked up at him slyly. "Okay, but we can't be seen. I'm supposed to be studying and they'll never let me live it down if they knew you and I were...well...um..."

"Fornicating?" He placed a nibbling kiss on her neck as she chuckled. "Fucking like bunnies?" His kisses trailed lower, pausing to look deeply into her eyes. "Making love?"

She blushed and hid her face in the curve of his neck, her arms tightening as her lips trembled against the skin just above his collar.

"Would it be so bad if they knew we were together?" he asked softly. Startlingly, her answer meant more than he would have imagined just a few days before. No woman had ever had such a strong claim on his emotions. "Do I embarrass you?"

That sounded way too vulnerable, but he couldn't call the words back. He brazened it out, glad when her eyes lifted and her soft palms caressed his stubbled cheeks.

"Never, Ezekiel. I just..." she seemed to search for the right words. "I've never felt this way before." His heart soared. "I just want to keep it to myself-to ourselves-for a little while. I want to savor it. Savor this. Savor you." She kissed him sweetly on the mouth, a light brushing of the lips. "Do you truly mind?"

"Not when you put it like that." He bent to sweep a light kiss across her luscious lips. "I think I can get us to the ship without being seen. I like a challenge." He growled and bit her earlobe playfully, making her laugh. "Let's go."

* * * *

Zeke was on her as soon as he set the shield. Within moments they were both naked and panting on the deck inside the main hatch. He couldn't even wait to get to his cabin, that's how strong the hunger for her gripped him. She was a need deep inside, a thirst that would never be quenched.

Zeke slid home, his hard body on top of her this time. His eyes followed her every move, her every emotion as it crossed her lovely face, riding hard but slow, in and out. He took his time now that he was where he wanted most to be in the universe. Where he belonged.

"Do you feel what you do to me, baby?" Angela moaned softly and closed her eyes, but he wouldn't allow it. He wanted her to know who was fucking her, who was part of her. "Look at me, Angel. Open your eyes."

Her eyes flickered open and she gasped, going stiff beneath him as her hands came up to cover her breasts and her eyes fixed in fright on something over his shoulder. Instantly alert, Zeke looked back and cursed.

"Dammit, Mike. Give us a minute here, will you?" He would not stop now. He couldn't.

"I thought you said no one could bother us once the shield was set." Angela was tense beneath him as he continued to move in her. Mike's appearance had probably killed a bit of the mood for her, he realized, slowing to give her time to adjust.

"None of your people, certainly, but I hadn't counted on Mike getting here so fast. Only one of my brothers would be so crass as to intrude on our fun." Instead of leaving, Michael, the cad, crouched down next to them, his eyes dancing with mischief.

"Go away, Mike. Go find your own girl. There are plenty of submissive females here that would welcome your services."

"Oh, I think your little lady might be a bit more submissive than you think, Zeke." Mike reached out to stroke her hair back from her face and Zeke growled. Mike just ignored him. "You like being watched, don't you, sweet?"

Zeke felt the clamping of her internal muscles around his cock, and the widening of her eyes told the rest of the tale. Mike was right. She was even wetter than she'd been when Mike walked in. Zeke wasn't sure if he liked her response to his brother or not, but he knew he would do anything to bring her pleasure. Her joy was his only concern.

"What do you say, Zeke? You need some help with her? You Riskers don't know the first thing about taming a filly."

Angela's narrowed eyes and gripping hands on his neck told their own story. "I like Ezekiel just fine, and I'm not a horse that needs taming." Her words came in short panting breaths as her passions rose again. Zeke liked the way she defended him and followed willingly as he neared the summit of passion once more. Mike had startled her and challenged her, but it was Zeke who made her whole. He just knew it. Or maybe he just prayed it was so, but either way he thought he could read it in her lovely face as she turned her lips up for his kiss.

Zeke pulled back, leaving her flat on her back on the floor while he held her legs out to either side of his hips, sitting up now with his dick firmly planted within her tight hole. He had an idea. It was a naughty one, but the Sons of Amber were up for all kinds of sexual hijinks at any time of the day or night. He and Mike had played this game before as a matter of fact, and he couldn't think of anyone he'd rather have here with them for this experiment. Of all the Sons of Amber, Mike was his closest friend.

Zeke wanted to push Angela's boundaries, to see how far she would go. He wanted to bring her pleasure, the likes of which she had never known, and make her realize he was the only man who would ever cherish her so deeply, prize her so highly. He wanted to make her come and come, then come again. Only then would he take his own pleasure.

"You know," he slid his gaze from her flushed face to Mike, "I think I could use a little help here, brother."

Mike's eyes lit up with anticipation. "Really?" He shifted his stance a bit. "And what can I do for you?"

"Well, see, I need someone to play with her clit while I fuck her senseless." Zeke's gaze challenged hers as she gasped. He could feel her pussy clamping down around his cock and he could feel the gush of excitement that followed. She was more into this than she let on. "Do you think you could help with that?"

Mike turned to look at her, moving one big hand to caress her tight nipple almost absently. Zeke felt her shiver with desire at the other man's touch.

"Can I play with these pretty tits, too, Zeke? I'd like to know what's off limits and what's not before we start."

Zeke caught and held her eyes. "Tell us, Angel. If I promise to guide you and let no harm come to you, is anything off limits? Will you take us both, any way I see fit? Do you trust me?"

* * * *

Angela thought she was about to scream, but she ruthlessly bit it back. She was not a screamer. The scandalous ideas of these two devastating men wound her passions higher than ever before. She wanted Ezekiel. She loved Ezekiel. But, this darkly arrogant brother of his was stirring lust in her as well. She didn't understand it at all, but her pussy sure seemed to want to let them both have at her.

She didn't understand what it was about them-or rather, about Ezekiel-that made her want to let go of every inhibition and trust him with her very life. She did trust him, though, she realized. She would follow him to the ends of the galaxy and back, if he let her. She could deny him nothing and knew that he cared on some level for her as well. He wouldn't let any harm come to her if it was within his power to prevent it. She was safe with him.

Breathing deeply, she answered the plea in his eyes.

"I trust you, Ezekiel."

His satisfied smile stole her breath. Ezekiel pulled out and Michael's hard arms lifted her as if she weighed nothing at all. Her head whirled as he carried her quickly into Ezekiel's cabin. Michael apparently knew the layout of the ship fairly well, for not once did his steps falter.

He looked down at her, his harsh face lit with desire as he whispered for her ears alone. "I'm Michael, by the way. I knew you were special the moment I saw you on the end of that transmission. I've never seen Zeke so happy." Zeke moved up to the bed then, four lengths of flexible rope dangling from his big hands. Her breath caught in ther throat when she saw them, and the heated expression on his face.

"I thought we could try these." Zeke grinned devilishly as he handed the ropes to Michael. A look passed between the two Sons of Amber that made her mouth go dry and her insides quiver.

"Give her a quick climax first, then we'll tie her up," Mike agreed with a knowing nod. This man was a connoisseur of women, it was easy enough to see. What had she done, agreeing to whatever they wanted? For a moment she thought of backing out, but then Zeke climbed between her thighs and started to play with her sensitive bud. All thoughts of fleeing left her mind as wetness seeped from her core, making her as ready as she'd ever been. So close now to orgasm, it would take little to make her come. He knew it, too. She could tell by the glint in his smiling eyes.

"There's something you need to know about Mike, Angel. He's a Dominant."

"Um...what?" It was hard to concentrate with him touching her like that, but she tried her best. A sudden thought occurred as she tried to puzzle out his words. "Oh. Do you mean he likes to be on top?"

Both men laughed, but not in a mean way. Zeke was driving her higher with his teasing touches, making it even harder to take in what he was saying, but she struggled to try.

"Oh, she's precious, Zeke. I can see why you want her." Mike's words sounded more admiring than teasing, so she knew they weren't laughing at her. Not that any of that would have mattered at the moment. As it was, she could barely breathe through the spiking pleasure as Ezekiel touched her just the way she needed.

"No, sweetheart." His voice was gentle as he brought her closer and closer to the peak. "When Dr. Waithe designed us, she made different types of males. Some are Pioneers, some are Moderates, some are Risk Takers, like me, and then there are also a quite a few Doms, like Michael. They like to dominate sexually, and there are many women who want and need to submit. You've already taken the first step by agreeing to this. I'm going to let him tie you up and give you pleasure, but ultimately you're mine, Angela. Never forget that." He lowered his lips to suck on her clit. "Your mine!" he whispered fervently against her straining flesh just a moment before he bit down gently, using his lips. She came under his mouth, fingers, and tongue with a wave of pleasure that wrenched a short, keening cry from her throat.

"Not bad, little brother," Michael commented from beside the bed, looking down on them, "but I'll bet we have her screaming before the night is through."

Zeke levered himself up off her and grinned. "I bet I can make her scream with pleasure first."

Mike reached across her body to shake Zeke's hand and seal the wager. She could barely believe these two magnificent men were competing to make her come loudest. It would be childish if it weren't so darn stimulating. She had just come, but already her fires were lighting again. Only Zeke had ever been able to do that for her, and now he was introducing her to something altogether new with the addition of his friend into their loveplay. She didn't know if she could handle it. She didn't even know if it was right, but she vowed to see where it would lead.

Zeke had staked a claim just now, a claim that made her feel warm and loved inside, where it counted. She trusted him. He would be her guide into this new, unexpected ecstasy.

"Are you ready for more?" Zeke asked gently as Mike tugged on her arms, tying one, then the other, to little rings placed strategically along Zeke's large bed. Funny, she'd never questioned those little rings when she'd seen them before, but now she had a sneaking suspicion the bed had been built with just this sort of thing in mind. It was scandalous! And very exciting.

Mike's touch was a little rougher than Zeke's, his hands demanding, but he never hurt her. He pulled and pushed her around as he tied her, making her feel small and vulnerable in a delicious sort of way, but he seemed always aware of his strength and mindful that he not be too rough with her tender skin. She liked that. She liked even more the way Zeke's gaze followed every line of her body, every movement as his brother tied her securely to the sinful bed.

"She's got great tits and a shapely ass." His hands stroked over her as he spoke, firing her senses even further. "A fine looking bit of pussy you've got here, Zeke." Mike talked to Ezekiel as if she weren't there. Somehow the idea of them talking over her in such crude terms was exciting rather than insulting. She could tell from the sparkle in Mike's dark eyes that he knew it, too.

Mike settled between her splayed thighs and she tensed for a moment of delicious anxiety as he touched her intimately for the first time. His touch was different than Ezekiel's, stronger and nearly intimidating. He knew what he was doing with a woman's body and zeroed in on what he wanted. It was exciting and a little scary, but Zeke took her face in his strong hands, soothing as he bent over her for a deep, almost drugging, kiss.

While Zeke kissed her, Michael swept his blunt fingers through her folds, swirling and dipping in ways that made her squirm. Her hips nearly lifted off the bed when he plunged one long finger inside her and he pulled out immediately, slapping her pussy in reproval, making her jump again. Zeke left off kissing her to look down her body with an open, lusty grin.

"Don't move, wench, or I'll have to spank you."

"Spank me?" Her breathless voice sounded alarmingly aroused even to her own ears as Mike tapped out a light, teasing rhythm on her distended clit. She sobbed as the fire within her spiraled higher.

"You like that, pussycat? I'll give you more, but you have to hold still."

"I can't!"

He stopped petting her and slapped her quick, hard enough to startle, but not quite hurt.

"You can and you will, disrespectful wench. When you speak to me, you will address me as Master, and you will not speak unless instructed to do so or questioned directly. Do you understand?" His fingers resumed their play on and around her clit.

"Yes." She nodded, holding Zeke's gaze and knowing from the flare of his expressive eyes that he was enjoying this every bit as much as she was.

A slap stung her excited pussy.

"Yes, what?"

She blushed as Zeke's gaze held hers, a fire leaping within. He wanted her to do this, she could tell, just as much as she wanted to do it. It surprised her really, that she could so willingly give herself up to this man-to Ezekiel. For although Michael was giving the orders this time, it was Ezekiel she wanted to please.

"Yes, Master." Her voice sighed out and Michael rewarded her by plunging two fingers deep into her hole. A moment later he licked her clit, driving her higher as Zeke stroked her nipples.

Michael stroked and sucked in rhythm until she was ready to explode. She did her best not to move, but the pleasure was so intense, she had a hard time of it. He stroked her until she cried out and then he bit down, nipping with just the right pressure on her sensitive clit as she exploded, sobbing softly as her climax blasted through her core.

The two men sat back, watching her as she slowly came back to herself.

"She didn't scream that time, Mike. You'll have to do better if you want to win our wager." Zeke's cock twitched as he looked down on his angel. She was so beautiful, so responsive, so trusting. He had no doubt she was his match in every way.

"Think she's ready for more?"

Zeke moved to her side, stroking her face as he looked down into her lovely eyes. "How are you doing, sweetheart?"

"I'm okay." Her beautiful smile nearly stopped his heart.

"Sir." Mike barked from her other side, making them both look up at him.

"What?" Angela seemed confused.

Mike moved onto the bed, positioning himself at her side, kneeling there, over her. He didn't touch, only looked over her ripe body with obvious pleasure.

"I'll have to punish you for your informality, wench. You will address Zeke as Sir while we're pleasuring you, and what do you call me?"

She gasped as Mike reached out and pinched her nipple. "Master."

Zeke leaned down to kiss her softly. "I told you he's a Dominant, Angel. He likes to play by his rules, but if you don't want to play anymore, just let me know, okay?" His words were low, near her ear, but he knew Mike heard. He didn't care. Angela came first, and he knew Mike well enough to know he would feel the same. Mike was a Dom, sure, but he preferred completely willing women. He would never force a woman to accept his terms if she didn't truly want to be dominated.

"No," Angela gasped as Mike's hands slid down over her body, "I'm good...Sir."

He pulled back and saw the sparkle of renewed passion and a bit of playful devilry in her pretty eyes. She gave him a sultry smile that made his own breath hitch and his cock twitch. By the Maker, she was beautiful! How he loved her adventurous spirit.

"How is she at sucking cock?"

Mike's rough question brought him back to the moment. He had to get inside her as soon as possible.

"She's skilled, Mike. I don't think you'll have any complaints."

Zeke stared across her body at his brother and

Mike nodded almost imperceptibly. This, he knew, was Mike's way of seeking silent approval of his plan. Zeke would let Mike fuck her mouth, but her pussy was his and his alone. Mike was a close enough friend that he knew without asking that although he was leading, Zeke was the ultimate authority on just how far this little scene would go. The only cum he wanted pumped into her perfect little pussy was his own. He'd give it to her again and again until she didn't remember what it felt like to not carry his seed inside her.

Mike moved closer to her head, opening the fly of his uniform and letting out the monster he kept in his pants. Mike was a big man. Though all of Amber's Sons were built on the large side to please a lady, Mike was bigger than most by about a half-inch of girth. His length was about the same as Zeke's so he knew Angela could handle him, but the width might stretch her pretty lips a bit. Zeke looked forward to seeing how she managed.

With a grin, he moved between her spread thighs once more. Her pussy was swollen with renewed need and wetter than ever as he dipped three fingers inside her tight passage. She moaned, looking down at him for a moment before Mike's hand brought her face back up so her eyes could meet his.

"We're going to fuck you now, wench. I'm going to fuck your mouth while my brother Zeke fucks your pussy." Zeke felt her walls tighten in anticipation as he slowly pumped his fingers in and out, preparing her. "I want your eyes on me, girl. I want you to look at me when you swallow my dick."

Without looking back, Zeke watched Mike feed her his wide cock. He felt her excitement in the clenching of her pussy around his fingers and the movements of her restless hips. She was hotter than ever, and ready for more by the time Mike had his entire length buried in her straining mouth.

Mike nodded to him once and Zeke removed his fingers, taking up his position and entering her by slow degrees as Mike started to stroke lightly in and out of her mouth.

"Suck it now, wench. Use your tongue." Mike directed her as Zeke slid home within her hot, wet depths.

"Damn, Mike. She likes fucking us both at once. Her pussy is clenching me like a fist."

Mike laughed like the master he was. "She's a good little girl, Zeke, and she likes cock." Mike pulsed in a little more quickly as her cheeks hollowed. "Oh, I'll have to think of some reward for you, wench. You suck me so well. Harder now, girl. Give it all you've got." Mike increased his pace, as did Zeke. Watching his angel suck off Mike's monster cock was making him hotter than he'd ever imagined. He could practically feel her lips around his own cock, remembering the pleasure she'd given him, knowing Mike felt the same amazing pleasure at this very moment.

Mike stopped moving and Zeke guessed what was coming next. Mike was a master of his own response.

"Tell me now if you don't want to swallow my cum, wench."

Mike backed off until just the tip of his cock was

inside her lips. She would be able to pull back completely if she didn't want him to come in her mouth, but she didn't pull back at all. Instead, she lifted her head up, eager for more. Mike growled at her response and pushed back into her mouth. Zeke knew it wouldn't be long before his brother came hard and long. He'd seen it before with other wenches they had shared.

Mike erupted with a shout as his hips jerked and he knew streams of cum were shooting down her throat. She swallowed hard and fast, but a lot of it slipped out to paint her chin and cheeks, and dribble down her neck in an erotic display. Zeke plunged in and out of her hot hole faster and faster, teasing her clit with his fingers until she spasmed around him. A moment later, he shot his cum up into her, over and over, on and on. His kind were made to have nearly endless supplies of sperm, and Angela was getting every last drop in both her pussy and her mouth.

Zeke thought he'd never seen anything hotter. He pulled out of her slowly and collapsed at her side for a short rest. Even a Son of Amber had to rest just a bit after coming so momentously. Zeke saw that Mike was stretched out at her other side and smiled wearily. His little angel had drained them both, and that was something not easily accomplished.

"You know," Mike observed dryly from the other side of the large bed, "I still didn't hear her scream."

"We're going to have to try again another day, brother." Zeke reached up to untie her arms and rubbed them gently as he lay bonelessly at her side, enjoying the afterglow.

Chapter Five

"So what brings you here, Mike? I didn't expect to see you."

"We're putting up a planetary shield and surveying for an orbital space station. Dr. Waithe wants to set up the tightest possible security around this colony. I escorted her down here to meet with the elders."

Both men were sated and a bit weary, sitting in the small lounge outside the cabin while Angela slept within. Uneasy thoughts bothered Zeke. He needed this time to talk to one of his brothers about the odd things occurring within him. Mike was one of his closest friends, and he knew he could trust the other man with his confidences.

"Dr. Waithe's in full protective gear, huh? Knowing our Amber, she's not going to be comfortable in it for long. Will you have to shuttle her back or did you bring others with you?"

"Only Sons are allowed down here right now. We're the only ones they can be sure won't carry the jit virus to infect these folks. Dr. Waithe took the chance because she wanted to verify the status of the colony for herself before going any further." Mike checked his chronometer. "But, to answer your question, Gabe will shuttle her back if I ask him.

Why?"

"Mike," Zeke ran a frustrated hand through his hair, "something's different in me. I don't understand it, but ever since I opened my eyes and saw Angela standing there, I don't want any other woman. Only her."

Michael sighed heavily. "I thought so." Zeke was startled by Mike's knowing tone. "You're not the first of our kind to tell me this. Dr. Waithe is aware of it. She's studying the phenomenon, trying to figure it out, but I don't think she's ever going to find a scientific explanation for it. I've seen it happen to two of my best men in the last few months. They each found one special woman and they don't want to perform with any others. Sure, they still make their donations to the sperm banks, but they just don't want to fuck any other woman than their special girl."

"Who were they? What happened to them?"

If this condition were spreading, Dr. Waithe would want to take action. She wasn't one to sit idly by and let her plans be ruined by some random anomaly. He only hoped she hadn't resorted to desperate means to keep her Sons on track with her goals.

"Mark and Todd."

Zeke recognized the names. "They're both Moderates. Have you heard of any other Riskers being affected?"

"You're the first I've heard of, Zeke. But you can stop worrying. Dr. Waithe keeps them under observation but they've both been permitted to cohabit with their women and are raising families.

Can you imagine it, Zeke?" A quiet wistfulness entered his voice. "They're actually raising their own sons. I visit them both from time to time and they're happier than I've ever seen them."

"So you think there's a chance I'll be allowed to stay with Angela?"

"More than a chance, my friend. This colony will need a few of us here on the surface to help them get up to speed with the tech we'll be giving them, among other things. I wouldn't be surprised if our Amber sees the wisdom in letting you live here with your girl. The people here already know you after all, and they seem to like you, though why I can't imagine." Mike chuckled as he rose to his feet. "I'm going to check on Dr. Waithe and see what's up. I'll make the recommendation to her that you be assigned here permanently, if you want. As far as I'm concerned, this duty station is yours, but since you're a Son, we have to clear it with Dr. Waithe first."

"I know." Zeke stood and held out his hand for a shake and quick hug. "And thanks, Mike. For everything."

Mike headed for the companionway, but paused as Zeke asked one final question.

"What do you think is happening to me and our brothers, Mike? If there's no scientific explanation, what could it be?"

Mike chuckled softly as an unfamiliar, almost envious feeling came over him. "I've read up on our ancestors, Zeke. In all the years of humanity's history and all the scientific advances they made, not one scientist or researcher could ever explain the phenomenon known as love." Mike slapped a hand on the doorframe. "I'd say you're in love with the girl, and if I'm not much mistaken, she loves you in return."

Mike left, whistling as he sauntered down the companionway. He'd given Zeke a lot of answers, but quite a few questions, too. How could he really know if he was in love with Angela? He didn't know what love was. It was something they hadn't covered in his accelerated training sessions. It had been assumed there would be no room for love in the life of one of the Sons of Amber.

He'd been designed to be a stud, providing service for any female who wanted it, supplying sperm for the next generation of babies. He hadn't been designed to find one woman and settle down the way their human ancestors had done before the virus. He didn't know if it was even possible that he could, but he was a Risk Taker, after all, and he was willing to risk everything for a chance at happiness with Angela.

He turned back towards the door to his sleep chamber, only to find her blinking up at him through teary eyes.

"Is it true?" Angela asked, something like hope filling her wide eyes. "Do you love me?"

In that moment, all of Zeke's questions were answered. If ever a man loved a woman, he loved Angela. He moved slowly forward to take her unresisting body into his arms.

"I do." He placed tender kisses all over her face. "I love you with all my heart, my angel."

"Oh, Zeke!" she gasped as he nipped his way down her neck. "I love you so much!"

Warmth flooded his heart. A pure, beaming, light of joy and radiant hope filled him. He wanted it all in that moment. He wanted her forever, bound to him and him to her. If it were at all possible, he would make it happen, he vowed.

"Do your people still have marriage ceremonies?" he paused in his kisses to ask. Slowly, she nodded. "Then," he took a moment to kneel down on one knee, holding her hand and looking up into her radiant face, "will you marry me, Angela? Will you be my wife?"

Hope, joy and love lit her sparkling eyes. "I will."

She laughed and cried at the same time, shrieking when he stood and lifted her up in his arms, twirling her around the cabin. It was a long time before they left the ship, going back to the settlement to tell the others their happy news.

* * * *

A few days later, they were married and given a traditional wedding feast according to the customs of Angela's people. But only after a long talk with Mother Rachel and Dr. Waithe. Zeke was eventually granted permission to marry his love, but both women had to give their blessing first. Rachel was easy to convince. It was Amber who put up more of an argument.

"But Zeke, are you certain?" Dr. Waithe had asked gently, her voice a little tinny through the speaker on her environmental suit. She couldn't risk contaminating the settlement, so she had to wear the slim suit that provided her own air supply. "You know why you were created, and the goals we have for saving our species."

Surprisingly, it was Rachel who stepped in. "He can still fulfill his role in your plan, Doctor. But why should he and Angela be denied happiness while he does so?"

"Doctor Amber," Zeke pled his own case, "I love Angela and she loves me. I never expected anything like this to happen, but it has and now I know I'll never be complete without her in my life. I'll still do my part to save the human race. I know my duty and the contribution I can make. I don't take that lightly, but I also know I need Angela."

Doctor Waithe sighed audibly, but Zeke took her soft smile behind the clear bubble of her suit's headpiece as a good sign. "Oh, Zeke. You're not the first man to fall in love, and I doubt you'll be the last." She reached up and cupped his cheek with her gloved hand, the maternal gesture surprising him. "I just never expected my boys to want to marry. I guess I should have thought about it, but I didn't."

"It's hard to let them leave the nest, isn't it?" Rachel moved up behind Amber.

The doctor chuckled. "I never really thought of myself as a clingy, overprotective mother." Amber turned to share a laugh with Rachel, who nodded understandingly.

"Every woman has it in her to protect her young. Ezekiel is your son as much as if you had carried him in your womb. The connection between you is strong and will not diminish."

Oddly it was Rachel who reassured the brilliant geneticist. Zeke watched in awe as the two women grew teary eyed discussing his wedding plans.

"You'll have to stay here for the time being, of course," Amber said, businesslike once again. "But we have to leave a contingent here anyway for the colony's protection, so that works out fine. I'll still want sperm donations every cycle, just like your brothers who'll be stationed here."

Rachel chuckled and winked at him. "I'm sure Sister Angela will have no objection to helping him with that."

All three laughed and the atmosphere relaxed. Amber stepped right up to him and took his hand.

"I want you to be happy, Zeke. You're a special young man and I want only the best for you."

Zeke squeezed her hand. "Angela is the best. You'll see."

And so permission was granted and Zeke was allowed to marry his unexpected love. Mike stood up as Zeke's best man, while Agatha filled the role of Angela's bride's maid. Amber and Rachel sat beside each other, both beaming as a stately, older, male priest recited the traditional words that would join Zeke and his angel forevermore.

* * * *

"I never expected this," Amber said a short while later to Rachel as they shared a moment of quiet before she had to leave.

"I know."

"Is it true you can see the future?"

Rachel tilted her head. "And do you, a woman of science, believe in such things?"

Amber's eyes narrowed. "I've seen many things in my time, and I've studied the human brain in some detail. I know there are still many things we cannot explain about psi abilities and that they do exist in some rare cases. I also know that the population of Espia had more than its share of psychic phenomena before the virus."

Mother Rachel nodded deeply. "We are the Order of Chion. All of our ancestors had some psychic ability when they left Espia for this planet, but it does not always breed true. Some of us have the abilities of our ancestors and some do not."

"But you do." It wasn't a question.

Again, Rachel nodded. "I have foreseen an end to this plague, and many happy marriages among your Sons. The only advice I can offer at this time is to not stand in their way. The love they find with the women lucky enough to claim them is hope for our future, Amber. There is a solution out there, and you will see it in your lifetime. Your Sons will play their role, but unexpected aid will come and when it does, you need to remember your goals, not the tragedies of yesterday. You must get past your anger and look to the future-as must we all."

Doctor Waithe thought on the seer's words for a long moment. Rachel offered hope, but intimated great changes ahead, especially for her Sons. If she was to be believed, they would start to marry in greater numbers. Amber had to make new calculations and try to anticipate what this unexpected development might do to her carefully laid plans.

"I'll take your words to heart, Mother Rachel.

Thanks for giving me hope." She turned to go, knowing her ship was waiting for her to depart.

"Just remember, Doctor," Rachel called softly after her, "Fate plays a much larger role in our existence than you might envision. Do not discount the power of destiny, or that of the most unstoppable force in the universe... love."

* * * *

And later that night, Zeke finally won his bet. He made his angel scream with pleasure.

Part Two: Michael

Chapter One

Michael Amber couldn't believe the ineptitude of the woman. The so-called General on the other end of the comm had obviously been promoted through the ranks due more to her prowess at schmoozing politicians than any real ability on her part. But Mike didn't play that game. He'd lay this idiot out in the clover, general, political crony, or not.

"Smithson-"

"Sir," the gentle voice at his side calmed him almost instantly, "perhaps you'd care to take the comm from General Smithson in your office."

He'd been *that* close to blowing his stack in front of the entire chain of command in a full-out Dominant rage. Commandant Michael Amber normally controlled his baser passions in front of other people, but every once in a while he'd succumb to one of the near-berserker states that sometimes plagued Dominants like himself. Not often, but every once in a while.

His Executive Officer-XO for short-Colonel Leah Blackfoot, had seen him in towering rages before, but she'd never backed away. No, this small woman was more fearless than a platoon of jit'suku warriors. She faced him down and tamed his inner beast with just a few well-placed words.

She was magic.

Curtly, he nodded at Leah. "Just so." Drawing himself to his full height-almost a full foot taller than Leah's willowy form-he headed for his private office, motioning her to follow. He didn't quite trust himself to talk to the idiot general without Leah there to mitigate his temper.

It had been like that almost from the beginning. Leah had been assigned to his staff about two years before and, after an initial getting-to-know-each-other period, they'd worked together like a well-oiled machine. She was the most organized, skilled, and naturally attuned woman he knew. She was also gorgeous, but he tried his best not to think of her in any kind of sexual way. More often than he liked, though, he'd find himself watching her...wondering.

Michael was a Son of Amber - a genetically engineered male designed with the express purpose of repopulating the human race. The jit'suku enemy had launched a bio-weapon years ago, systematically killing off almost all human males. Some women became ill as well and were left sterile or worse.

A few dedicated geneticists, led by Dr. Amber Waithe, had stepped up to the challenge. She and her team devised a plan to restore the balance, engineering a group of males who were immune to the jit virus. Known as Sons of Amber, these men also bred about ninety percent male offspring. They'd been designed so each successive generation would yield more female offspring until normalizing somewhere around fifty-fifty several generations down the road. By that time, it was hoped the human race would be back on its feet as a species.

But Michael Amber was one of the first. He and

his brothers had been designed in several discrete groups. Some were Risk Takers, designed to weigh the odds and take calculated risks that others would not. Some were Pioneers, given the skills and predispositions to conquer new frontiers in every field of human endeavor. Some were Moderates, designed to be the backbone of society, even-tempered and rock steady in character, and some were Dominants like Michael.

Dominant personalities were meant to lead in all aspects of life. It made them great military commanders, law enforcers, and the like, but it also gave them Dominant tastes in everything they did. In Michael's case, he was probably one of the most dominant of the Doms. He'd worked his way up to Commandant of the military forces in this sector. He led, and everyone followed. Just the way he liked it.

The way he *needed* it, actually. It was part of his physiology and his psyche. He needed to dominate the way others needed to breathe. And he needed to dominate sexually as well, though never to the point of violence. Violence was something Mike reserved for his enemies. He'd killed his fair share of jit'suku soldiers in his climb to the top of his chosen profession, but he never gloried in it. He just did what he had to do to protect his own. It was that simple.

Mike also understood the value of working with people. He had good working relationships with all his command staff and his people respected him. That was important to him. He cultivated friendships with his staff, who were mostly female, though he discouraged any interaction or discussion of a sexual nature.

While he still made regular deposits to the sperm banks, and made personal visits to as many civilian ladies as his schedule allowed, he never had sex with his subordinates. For one thing, it wouldn't be fair to take advantage of his position of authority. For another, he had definite sexual tastes and proclivities that required the full understanding of his partner. How could he be certain the woman consented out of her own desire or out of some misguided aspiration to get a promotion by doing whatever he wanted, regardless of her own needs? Mike couldn't take the chance, so military women were off-limits.

If any woman tempted him to break his own rule, though, it was Leah. Still, she'd never once given him any indication she desired him sexually. Perhaps that was why he found her so comfortable to be around. She was his friend, his confidant, his stabilizer when his Dominant genetics threatened to push him a bit too far.

Like right now.

Michael made sure the hatch was closed tight before switching the comm to his personal viewer. Leah remained just out of range of the viewer, but well within his personal sphere. He could see her, read her expressions, and feel her calming energy. He didn't quite understand how it all worked, but something about this woman made him a better leader. She made him stop and think through his decisions, made him want to be the best man he could possibly be. In short, she was an invaluable influence and if he had any say in the matter, she'd be part of his personal staff for the duration of his career. She was a keeper.

* * * *

Leah watched Michael Amber handle the moronic woman who had somehow been promoted to general. Michael was like no man in her experience. Leah was in her late thirties and had been briefly married before the jit attack that killed her husband and all her male relatives. She knew full well what Michael Amber and his 'brothers' were. They'd been designed in a lab and grown under accelerated conditions. They were genetic constructs, but she knew first hand from her dealings with Michael that he had a deep, feeling, sensitive soul.

He was one of the most complex and courageous men she had ever known. Her own brothers had been military men before the virus, as had her father and many of her ancestors. She came from a line of warriors, and she knew and understood the mindset. Michael was as good as the best of them-and then some. He was superior to most other men she'd known in almost every way. Especially in the way that mattered most. He was completely immune to the jit virus.

And so were his children.

Leah had wanted a large family, but her husband of just a year was killed early on by the virus. That was years ago now, and few men were left. There were no marriages in the old sense now, only Sons who would flit from woman to woman like bees pollinating flowers, never settling on just one to live with and love. Leah wasn't entirely certain the Sons knew what love was. They hadn't been raised in a normal family, after all. They'd been incubated and their growth accelerated so they were 'born' in adolescence, just as their reproductive systems came online. A few years of training after that, and they were loosed on society.

Their sperm was collected and made available to all the human worlds so women who wanted to conceive could go to fertility clinics and be impregnated with the sperm of the Son of their choice. Catalogs containing short bios and images of all the Sons were found in such places so women could have some say in what their children might look like or what traits they might inherit from their fathers.

It was all too clinical, but there was little choice. Higher ranked women like Leah could also opt to reserve time with one of the Sons as scheduling allowed, to try to get pregnant the old fashioned way, but that seemed even worse to her.

Nearing forty, Leah was starting to really worry about just how and when she would finally start her family. She wanted a baby. A little boy to raise and nurture. She wanted it desperately, but since coming to work for Michael Amber, all too often when she pictured her son, he had Michael's dark hair and flashing blue eyes. She could easily imagine the boy she would dote on and love with all her heart, as she couldn't afford to love his father.

Michael was a Son of Amber. He was also one of the most influential and successful of the Sons. Not a man who could settle with one woman-ever. Such daydreams were useless and could be dangerous to a woman who worked with the tempting man, day in and day out. She knew Michael depended on her. He might even feel some kind of affection for her, but he would never feel the love she desired with every fiber of her being.

She'd been married. She knew what young love felt like, and she missed it. Sometimes she ached for the half-forgotten feel of her husband's arms around her. It was so long ago, she barely remembered him now. Sometimes it all seemed so pointless.

The time was drawing near when she'd have to make a decision. Either she stayed working with Michael, watching him, wanting him, and knowing she could never have him, or she would quit. She'd resign her commission and visit the fertility clinic, choosing Michael's seed to produce her baby boy.

The choice was a cold one, but the result would warm her heart for the rest of her life. Michael's baby couldn't help but be a reflection of the great man she'd come to know…and love.

The thought jarred her as he ended the comm. Michael sighed heavily and sat wearily at his desk.

"Thanks. I definitely owe you one for that, Colonel."

Leah gathered her wits and sat as he indicated the chair in front of his desk. "Anytime, sir."

"Smithson ought to be court-martialed for her actions."

Leah chuckled dryly. "She's too well connected. They'll never go after her."

He sighed. Leah had to stop herself from staring at his massive shoulders as he sat back in his chair.

The man was all too appealing for her peace of mind. Lately it had gotten harder and harder to ignore his incredibly masculine attributes. Ever since she'd decided she would have his baby, she found she couldn't look at him with the same detachment she'd cultivated since first being assigned to his staff.

"It's disgusting."

"You've got that right," Leah muttered, thinking more of her wayward thoughts and inability to focus on the task at hand than what he was actually talking about. It was time to quit thinking of Michael as a stud and concentrate on the work they had yet to accomplish. They had a lot to get through today and this little run-in with an idiot general had sidetracked them enough. "You'll be lucky if she doesn't start trash talking you among the other generals."

A cold look entered his icy blue eyes. "Let her try."

A shiver coursed down her spine and she understood what the gossips meant when they talked about Michael Amber's death glare. He'd become famous among the soldiers fighting to protect humanity for his skill and intense methods. Leah had never actually fought beside him, but she caught glimpses of the deadliness of the man every now and again.

She'd trained in the gym with him just once, early on in her tenure as his Executive Officer. After that one, sweaty, dangerous run-in, she'd avoided being in the gym with him ever again. He was deadly with his hands and he moved like a serpent-sinuous, strong and lethal.

His physique was impeccable. His musculature

made her mouth water in a way it should not for a man who was firmly off limits. His eyes were intent, his concentration total. He'd impressed her, and before the virus she'd been exposed to the best of the best of military men in her own family and tribe. She thought she was used to his kind of man, but Michael Amber was in a class by himself.

"The jits are getting too cocky, though. More and more of them are turning pirate and raiding fringe colonies, stealing supplies and women. It's got to be stopped."

Leah shook herself, trying to concentrate on what he was saying rather than the scandalous thoughts about her boss that came more often of late. "I agree. Especially when there might still be undiscovered pockets of uninfected humans out there like those Ezekiel found."

Mike nodded, turning to his read-outs. "Something's got to be done. Do you have the assignment roster for our intel scouts?"

She accessed her handcomp, which never really left her side. It contained all the pertinent data she might need in a hurry and connected her with other banks where she could access all kinds of things within a few moments. She lifted the small pad from her hip and switched it on from standby mode. A cheery blue glow greeted her.

"Anyone in particular, sir?"

Mike's glacial blue eyes narrowed. "Zeke would have been perfect for this, but he's retired." He was thinking aloud, a habit she'd grown used to over the years. "I need a Risker for this kind of mission. One who's available now or will be in the next week or two?"

"Male, then?"

Mike nodded. "A Son could possibly blend in with the jits."

She started to comprehend what he had in mind. Few humans had ever reported seeing a jit'suku female, so if Michael wanted to infiltrate their ranks, it had to be done by a male. Only a Risker would be fool enough to try, and only a Risker had any odds at all of succeeding. She consulted her lists.

"Silas and Tyron are free now. Smith, Hauer, and Billy come free within the next two weeks."

"All right. Comm Ty and see if you can get him here tomorrow for a little strategy session. Last I heard, he had some pretty good contacts on the outer rim."

"Yes, sir." She made a note to contact the man on one of their high-security channels.

Chapter Two

Tyron arrived on the interplanetary shuttle the following work period. He hefted his satchel over one shoulder and headed for the military wing of the station. It would be good to be on a mission again. He was getting restless more often lately, but doing a special job for his brother Mike was just the ticket to take him out of the doldrums.

His golden hair was a bit longer than standard military cut, earning him a few looks from the uniformed women bustling around. They knew darn well what he was, if not exactly who he was. Men were so rare, few seldom ventured off their home worlds, and even fewer took the risk of working actively in the military on one of the more vulnerable stations. No, the only males seen up here were Sons of Amber going to and fro on various missions, both military and civilian.

Atlantia Station was the most heavily defended orbital platform, seeing as it served as this sector's HQ. His brother, Commandant Michael Amber, ran the show from this orbiting gun platform and oversaw the defense of every planet, ship, station and colony in the sector. It was a big job and Ty didn't envy Mike the enormous responsibility, but he knew there was no better man for the job. He admired Michael and counted him among his closest friends.

Ty would do just about anything for Michael, and he knew the feeling was mutual. They'd grown up together-at least as much as Sons "grew up" after coming out of the incubator. They'd been in the same instructional classes and had partnered for fighting exercises and other tasks. They worked well together, their skill sets complimenting each other and, more than that, they genuinely liked each other.

The same could not be said of all Sons, though most of them shared some basic comradeship simply because they *were* Sons. They were the only males of their kind and that bound them together somewhat.

Ty smiled at the women who watched him pass, winking at a few-either making dour faces smile or young cheeks blush. He liked women of all kinds, though lately he'd found his many encounters with the female kind lacking. He didn't understand it, and had no idea what he was looking for, but nevertheless, it was there. A vague sense of dissatisfaction.

Oh, he enjoyed the sex. Scratch that. He *loved* the sex. But he wanted something...more. What that 'more' was, he didn't quite know, but he was beginning to suspect, like some of his other brothers, he was looking for one special woman with whom to share his life.

He wasn't actively seeking her-he knew he had a job to do that precluded tying himself to just one woman-but he still felt the lack. Was it love he was missing? He didn't know. He wasn't sure he'd ever experienced love, but he was intrigued enough to consider the possibility, though he would never act on it. No, his duty lay in repopulating the human race. Even if there were one special woman out there for him somewhere, he couldn't commit to her and go against everything he'd been created to do. Better he go on these missions and do his duty, protecting the remnants of the human race and forget his foolish yearnings. Mike would help get his head screwed on straight. If there was one Son of Amber who always lived up to his responsibilities, it was Mike.

Ty found Mike's private apartment and announced himself at the door, which would relay the signal to those inside. Mike had to be off-shift at this hour, so Ty had come directly here, bypassing the office and more formal surroundings. Ty wasn't a formal man.

Mike answered the door with a drink in his hand and a look in his eye that said he'd had more than one. Ty was surprised. Mike had never been a drinker, or one to use a crutch of any kind. Dominant to the core, Michael was a straight shooter who muscled his way through life with both brawn and intellect.

"Rough day, brother?"

Mike leaned one arm up against the door frame and sighed.

"You could say that." He stepped back to allow Ty entrance. "Thanks for coming. What can I get you?"

Ty dumped his bag by the couch as he took a seat. Michael had nice living quarters-a bit Spartan for Ty's tastes-but still nice and comfortable. Big, solid furniture that he could sit in without worrying if he'd break it somehow, and strong enough to support his tall frame. Ty stretched his tired muscles as Michael moved to the sideboard where a number of decanters sat on a small tray with glasses.

"Some Scotch wouldn't go awry."

Michael poured the alcohol and handed a glass to Ty before collapsing into one of the overstuffed chairs placed in a grouping with the couch.

"I'm glad you could make it."

Ty sat back, savoring his first sip of the fine brew. "I'm always glad to help, brother. Truth be told, I've been a little restless lately. This kind of assignment ought to be just the thing."

"Leah filled you in on the details?"

Ty noted the odd tone of Michael's voice and it puzzled him. Mike was usually the steadiest of men. The slight waver when he spoke his XO's name concerned him.

"She sent me the pertinent facts. I can infiltrate out in that sector pretty easily. I've laid the groundwork for years. A few of the tamer pirates know me and will vouch for me with the others."

"That's good." Mike knocked back his drink and leaned his head against the back of the big chair, stretching out.

"You want to tell me what's wrong? Does it have something to do with Leah?"

That got Mike's attention. His eyes popped open and glared in Ty's direction.

"I'm not even going to ask how you figured that one out." Mike sighed heavily and his eyes closed again. "It's nothing. She's the best damned XO I've ever had."

"And the most beautiful. Not to mention capable."

"She is that," Mike agreed. "But she's beside the point."

"Maybe." Ty decided to let the matter of Leah drop. He'd seen them interact. There was more to that story than either one would admit, but he figured they'd sort it out in time.

"So what's this restlessness about? Want to change careers?" Mike knew him better than that, but Ty recognized the wry, almost teasing tone. He decided to come clean. Mike knew him well. He was also highly placed. Maybe he knew more about the situation with the Sons who'd found life mates than he'd let on.

"I think it has to do with those marriages lately. I never thought Zeke would take himself off the market."

"Yeah, I was a little surprised at first, but his Angela is one hell of a woman."

"You've met her then?"

Mike's eyes held a knowing gleam Ty recognized immediately. Every once in a while Sons gave each other a hand with a woman. It was rare, but they'd all done it a time or two. With the highly sexual way they'd been designed and raised, it seemed only natural for them to want to experiment with more daring forms of pleasure on occasion.

"Angela is perfect for Zeke. I think they'll have a happy life together."

"I hope you're right." Ty leaned forward on the couch. "Mike, do you think there's a woman for each of us? Lately I've been feeling…I don't know…a little incomplete. I feel something strange when I see some of our brothers partnering up with just one woman. Like maybe that's what I want."

"You got a special woman in mind?" Mike's eyes studied him.

"Maybe." Ty was reticent. "I don't really know what love is. But I think I want to find out."

"When you figure it out, let me know." Mike's eyes were haunted and Ty thought his brother might have a bit more knowledge than he realized.

They talked of the mission and set up lines of communication they could use. Leah had prepared a set of ident chips for Ty and they went through the details of the operation before Ty took his leave an hour or two later. He'd grab some sleep, then head out on the next shuttle. He had a job to do.

* * * *

That evening, Leah wrote out her letter of resignation the old fashioned way, as such things deserved, and left it on Michael's desk with a pang of regret for what could never be. She'd miss him-his rare smiles, his determination, his quick mind…and so much more, but she'd soon have his son to coddle and raise. He'd never know it, of course, but she'd cherish the child for his father's sake and for his own. It was her fondest wish to have a baby, and there was no doubt in her mind she wanted Michael Amber to be the father. She'd made her decision.

The only thing that could possibly have made it better was if she had the guts to actually ask Michael to do the deed himself. She knew she couldn't keep him, but spending even one night in his embrace would be a memory to last a lifetime.

But she didn't have that kind of courage.

For one thing, she didn't know how to ask for such an intimate favor. For another, she didn't want to ruin their easy friendship-which she hoped might continue from afar even after she left the service-with messy emotional entanglements. Michael had a strict rule about not having sex with any of his subordinates and she guessed it was because the man she'd come to know had more of a heart than even he realized. He genuinely liked the women who worked for him and he didn't want to hurt any of them. He was too astute not to realize the women he bedded often wished he could fall in love with them and stay forever.

But such was not his life and probably never would be. He was a Son. He had a job to do. He knew his duty and it was a vast one. He and the rest of the Sons had to spread their seed far and wide to save humanity from extinction. It was what he'd been created to do. He hadn't been engineered to settle with just one woman. It just wasn't in the cards he'd been dealt.

With a sigh of regret for what could never be, Leah left the letter on his desk and returned to her own office. She had to start setting the wheels in motion for her replacement. There were files to get in order and her belongings to remove. Her resignation wouldn't take effect for another few weeks, but this interim period had to be used to prepare for a seamless transition to a new XO for Michael-or, at least, as seamless as possible.

He'd probably never even notice the difference.

Chapter Three

Michael couldn't believe his eyes when he saw the old fashioned slip of paper on his desk the next morning. He read it twice before swearing a blue streak and jumping up from behind his desk. He stalked into Leah's office without even the courtesy of knocking.

"What the hell is this?" Michael waved the paper in front of her face as she sat calmly behind her desk.

"It's my resignation."

"I can see that." He threw the paper down in exasperation. "What I want to know is why? I thought you were happy here. Dammit, Leah, I can't do this job without you." Sighing, he sank into the guest chair in front of her efficient desk, slouching in an uncustomary pose of defeat. "I can't accept this."

"Sir," she began, but he stopped her words.

"Don't you think you've known me long enough to use my name-at least when we're alone?"

Leah folded her hands in front of her, a pained expression on her face. "All right. Michael." She sighed. "Look, I really do enjoy working with you, but with recent developments, you don't need me as much as you used to. I'm getting older and, to be perfectly honest, I want to have a child before I'm too old to enjoy it. That's why I want to leave the military. I want to have a family."

Her words stunned him. And angered him.

"And just who did you want to father your child, Leah?" His voice was deadly and low. Leah seemed lost in her daydream, though, her lovely eyes clouded over as she thought of something only she could see. She didn't realize the danger that had crept into the room with her words.

"I made an appointment at the fertility clinic for as soon as my final paperwork goes through."

That made him sit back. At least she hadn't scheduled time with one of his brothers. She was highly-ranked enough she could request time with a Son of Amber on pretty short notice, though she wouldn't be guaranteed which of the Sons she might get.

"But why quit? We still need you here, Leah, and many women work right up 'til their eighth or ninth month."

She cleared her throat, seeming a little uncomfortable, shuffling items unnecessarily on her desk. "I wanted to avoid any possible conflict of interest."

Mike sensed a victory, but he didn't quite understand it yet-at least, he didn't dare hope the odd thought he had might be true. "And just why would being pregnant create a conflict of interest?"

"Look, Michael, I'll come clean here. I respect you enough to give you the truth, no matter how uncomfortable it makes my last few days here." She took a deep breath, meeting his gaze with resignation, a becoming flush highlighting her high cheekbones. "When I made the clinic appointment, I requested..." She looked away, clearly flustered. "Damn, this is harder than I thought it would be, but you've a right to know."

"Tell me." His voice was low, commanding. He was all Dom in that moment, and she responded.

"When I made that appointment, I specifically requested your... um... semen be used for the implantation. I want you to father my baby. I admire your intellect, your decisive nature-all your abilities and attributes, really-and I couldn't think of a better candidate to father my little boy."

Mike just watched her. She grew nervous under his stare, but he needed time to regroup. She'd just pulled the rug out from under him, but in the best possible way. He took a moment to consider his options.

"I'm flattered," he said finally. "And honored." He lifted the resignation in his hands and quite deliberately tore it to shreds, placing them neatly on her desk. "I don't accept this." He enjoyed the dismay on her face as he stood and leaned over the desk, so close he could smell her unique perfume.

"I-"

"Cancel the appointment." His tone was soft, but the order in his words was clear. "If you want to have my child, I'll give him to you personally. No other way, Leah. I've wanted you for the past two years. I'm not going to wait any longer." As he spoke the words, he realized their absolute truth.

"Now just a minute!" She stood, outrage in her eyes, but he wouldn't allow it. He rounded the desk and caught her by the arms, dragging her against his body. His lips came down on hers and time ceased to exist. He'd wanted to kiss her from the moment he'd first laid eyes on her, but she never indicated even the remotest interest. Now, however, all bets were off. He could see the very real desire as she spoke, and taste the heated excitement in her kiss. She wanted him. Probably as much as he'd always wanted her.

"You're mine, Leah." He pulled away enough to whisper. "You have been since the moment I first saw you."

"Michael-"

He covered her lips with a light, chastising kiss. Everything had clicked into place when his lips first touched hers. All was right with the universe-at least, the microcosm of the two of them together. Now that he'd tasted her, he would never go back to the old, arms-length relationship. She was his. The sooner she came to terms with that-and with him-the better.

"You know I'm a Dom, Leah, but I've never dominated you in our working relationship, and I never will. I'll freely admit, though, I've wanted to dominate you in pleasure for as long as I've known you. I want to feel you come around me and I want to give you the greatest climaxes of your life. I want to imprint myself on you so you'll never, ever forget me."

She sighed, a small, defeated sound. "That's what I'm afraid of, Michael. I like you too much. I'm afraid..."

"Afraid of what, Leah? You're the bravest woman I know." His hand cupped her chin, raising her beautiful eyes to his.

She smiled softly and his heart clenched. "I don't

want to fall in love with you, Michael. I want your baby, but I don't want a broken heart."

"Would it help you to know that by resigning, you're already breaking my heart? I honestly don't think I can continue without you at my side, Leah. We're a team." He rubbed circles on her back as she relaxed in his arms. She felt like heaven against him. "There's no reason you can't stay with me for a while yet. We can work together during the day and work on the baby at night." He winked, making her smile. He took her response as a good sign. "When you get pregnant, you can continue to work as long as you like and even after the baby is born, I have no objection to your bringing him to work. In fact," his head quirked to the side as he thought of it, "I think I'd like that. I don't know any of my children. The chance to see one as it grows would be welcome, if you don't mind my taking an interest."

"Are you kidding?" She seemed surprised by his candor. "You're the father. Of course you can take an interest in him."

"That's not the way it's been 'til now."

She shocked him by reaching up to stroke his cheek. No woman had ever offered to comfort him before and he found the very idea of it intriguing, the feel of her soft hand, more special than anything he'd ever felt before. Leah was such a miracle to him.

"I've never said anything, but I think it's wrong the way they expect you to father all these babies, but never have a chance to raise any of them. I mean, I know it'd be impossible for you to know all your children, but why not at least a few? You could be such a good influence on a young boy."

He covered her hand with his own, loving the feel of her soft skin against his. "I'm glad you think so."

"I wouldn't have chosen you to be my baby's father if I didn't admire you, Michael. I just don't know if I-"

"What?" He had to coax her. She was blushing again and it charmed him.

"I don't know if I can be submissive. I'm not exactly a shrinking violet. Or hadn't you noticed?" She laughed at herself, charming him even more.

"You're a strong-willed, capable woman, but being sexually submissive doesn't require a weakling personality. In fact, I gain very little satisfaction from a meek woman's obedience. I can all too easily trample over a weaker personality. I know that much about myself, at least." He shrugged. "Which is why I've enjoyed your company for so long. You're the first woman who hasn't bored me to tears after a week or two, Leah. That's something unique in my experience." He pulled her closer, pressing his hardness against the soft V of her thighs. "I know I can make you want to follow my orders in the bedroom-or wherever we take our pleasure-and it will be pleasure, Leah. The greatest you've ever known, or will ever know. I can guarantee that."

Her breathless sigh thrilled him. He was getting to her. He knew it.

"I don't know, Michael." He loved the sound of his name on her lips. "I'm still concerned I won't be able to do what you want and I don't want to fight you."

He hugged her close. "I'll never force you, Leah.

There's no satisfaction in overpowering a woman. What I want from you is your willing compliance with my desires." He pulled back to look into her eyes. "I know you want me. I can make you want my dominance, too. Give it a try, Leah. Have dinner with me tonight. Let's see where it leads."

"Michael-"

"Come on, Leah. We've shared a thousand meals together."

"But this is different."

Mike cupped her ass audaciously with one hand as he grinned down at her. "Very different. I dare you, Leah. Take a chance."

* * * *

Michael Amber always could talk her into doing things against her better judgment. Well, to be fair, he never wanted her to do anything that was dangerous or could be harmful. He just had a way of getting what he wanted. She guessed it was part of his Dominant personality, and to be truthful, it didn't bother her much. In a way, it was sort of endearing.

That was the truly dangerous thing. This man was all too appealing. She knew it wouldn't take much to turn her admiration for him into something much more intimate. Everyone knew it was impossible to keep a Son of Amber for longer than it took to get pregnant, but so many women tried and failed.

Although there were a few stories making the rounds of gossip lately, and she knew for a fact that Ezekiel had been reassigned permanently to the newly discovered uninfected colony of Espians. It was rumored he had married and was living monogamously with one of the colony women. Oh, he still made the required sperm deposits so his DNA could go further in repopulating the human race, but he didn't make personal calls anymore and had been taken permanently off the reservation lists.

"I don't know, Michael." She'd never dared call him by name to his face, though it had crept into her mind more and more often.

His lips nipped at hers playfully. This side of him was new, and very exciting. She'd seen him in full Dom mode as he ruled most of the human fighting forces in this sector. She'd seen him weighted down by the burdens of his position and role. Her heart had gone out to him as time and again he sacrificed his own desires for the greater good of humanity, and she'd admired him for his steadfast determination to defeat their enemies.

This coaxing, cajoling, teasing hunk was something altogether new. His lips teased hers, his breath hot and sweet, mingling with her own. This man was born a Dom, but he was patient and kind in ways she never expected.

"Do it, Leah. You know you want to." He cuddled into her his chest, his cheek seeking her neck as he rubbed against her in the most delicious way. "Dinner. With me. What happens after that is wide open."

"But what about your rule? No fraternizing, remember?"

"Rules are made to be broken. Besides, you're the only woman under my command I've ever wanted to break that little unofficial rule with. No one else, Leah. Just you." He punctuated his words with small kisses to her face, teasing her until she smiled.

* * * *

"All right," she answered, finally. He wanted to pound the air with his fist in triumph, but refrained. "I'll have dinner with you tonight, Michael, but we'll discuss this. I won't be rushed into anything."

"No rushing." He nodded. "Gotcha." Pulling her closer, he kissed her, wanting to feel her response again and again. She was his. He knew it deep in his soul, though he didn't understand it at all. Now he just had to make sure she knew it, too. She would have his baby and he'd enjoy every moment of putting it in her womb and watching it grow. The very idea made something soft and fragile blossom in his sheltered heart. He didn't know quite what it was, but he definitely had his suspicions.

Chapter Four

Mike had a plan. He'd spent time breaking her in to his ways when she'd started as his XO two years ago. She'd been skittish at first, and it took him a few weeks to get her used to being around him and his manner of speaking-and sometimes barking orders-when he was in full Dom mode. Eventually, she'd come to anticipate his wants and needs and turned out to be the best XO he'd ever had.

That was only part of the reason he didn't want to lose her.

The rest had to do with little things. The way she moved. The way she spoke. The way she could talk him down from a Dominant rage with just a few well-placed words of caution and sense. The way her mind worked. The way she smelled of clean woman and daffodils. The way her hair swayed on the rare occasions she wore it down, and the way she smiled at him every so often as if he personally hung all the moons of Jupiter.

He couldn't lose her. Especially not after she'd conceived his child. He'd fathered many children, but this one would be special. This one in particular, he wanted to see gestate and be born, grow and change. He wanted to know and love this child as he knew and...loved...its mother.

The thought stopped him.

Did he love her?

Mike wasn't sure. He didn't really know what love was all about. It wasn't something he'd ever come across before personally. He'd seen a few of his brothers succumb, and longed to learn what it was that made one woman preferable to all the others. If there was such a woman for him, he hoped she was like Leah.

Hell, perhaps she *was* Leah. He'd be damned if he'd let her leave him now. First he had to know for sure whether these odd new feelings could really be love. That question had to be answered first, before anyone left or retired or resigned. Mike knew from his research, and from watching his brothers, that love was too important to let go.

So, he had a plan.

Like he'd done when she'd first signed on as his assistant, he would gentle her to his ways little by little. He knew the demands of a Dominant could be difficult on the uninitiated, but he couldn't change what he was born to be. His only hope lay in the idea that she could adapt to not only accept, but revel in the kind of pleasure he could give her.

He'd start slow. He'd start with the basics. Never had he looked so forward to just kissing a woman for hours on end.

And that's just what he'd do. He'd train her to hunger for his kiss, to want it more than her next breath, and then he'd move the next level. He'd break her in gently. Unlike the way he'd been introduced to sex and what it meant to be a Dominant.

Michael's first memory was of a woman's hand

on his cock. Awakened in adolescence from the incubator in which he'd been grown at an abnormally fast rate, Mike's first memory was of pleasure. He supposed there were worse things to remember, but he hadn't understood much of anything at that point. He only knew the amazing feeling of the woman's soft hand massaging his cock until he spewed.

When he'd come five or six times-enough to fill her sample collection units-she left him to sleep. By that time he was tired enough to fall into unconsciousness while the doctors ran their tests on his semen to see if their experiment was a success or not. To see whether he lived or died, essentially.

He had some muscle tone, thanks to the automated units that were designed to move his limbs and the rest of his body while he grew at an alarmingly fast rate in the incubator, but motor coordination had to be learned the old fashioned way. The first few months out of the incubator were an intense time of learning and growing, though his rate of growth eventually slowed almost to the stopping point. He'd been designed that way. He grew to adulthood quickly, then practically ceased to age so he'd have many productive years in which to do his ordained word of re-seeding the human population of the Milky Way galaxy.

He'd been subject to data downloads that worked-for the most part-to bring him up to speed with linguistic skills and book learning, but there was a great deal to be gleaned just from existing and interacting with the scientists and his brothers. They formed a family together and there were real, caring relationships among them.

Though at first they'd been kept separate, until they learned the role of sexuality. Just hatched from the incubators and knowing nothing but pleasure, most of the Sons tried to hump anyone who came into their chambers the first few weeks. It was a bit of a joke now, but the sad fact that the adolescent Sons were nothing more than sex machines when they were first born was an all too true urban legend.

When your first memory is pleasure, it's kind of hard not to want to repeat the sensation over and over...and over again, Mike thought with a small grin.

* * * *

Leah didn't know what to expect after the tumultuous events of the afternoon. She fussed over her hair, unsure what to wear for this...date. She hadn't been on a date since before the jit virus. Since before she was married. Women didn't date these days. For one thing, the men were few and far between. When you got one to yourself, you didn't waste time going to dinner and a movie. No, you kept him to yourself and enjoyed him while you could.

Michael had asked her to have dinner with him, but other than that, had given no indication of where they were going to eat, or whether she should wear her uniform or off-duty clothing. Nervous as she hadn't been for years, Leah decided to comm him to find out.

"Yes, Leah, what is it? Not chickening out on me, are you?"

"No, sir. I-" She faltered, feeling foolish.

"Its Michael when we're alone, remember?" His deep voice charmed her, even over the comm. "Unless I order you to call me something else."

The wicked purr in his words made her insides itch. She knew he was a Dom. He was designed to take charge, especially in sexual situations, but other than that, she was unprepared for just how far he might go in his Dominant games.

"Something else?" She couldn't help the words that escaped before she thought better of it.

He chuckled low, the sound stirring her womb. "Eventually. But we'll save that for later. Now why did you comm me? Not that I'm complaining."

"I wanted to know, uh, what time we were having dinner and where. I mean, should I wear my uniform, or-"

"Leah, sweetheart," he stopped her nervous words. "I was hoping you'd ask."

She knew that tone. "This was some kind of test?"

"Just a little one." He shrugged. "I wanted to know how you'd react. Would you come to me? Would you make assumptions without asking for my guidance? Or worse, would you forge ahead with some preconceived notion without considering my desires at all?" He smiled as her outrage grew. "I thought I knew you well enough after the past two years to judge your reaction, but I wanted to know for certain. It was a test of my own perceptions as much as it was a test of your reactions."

"I don't like being studied like a lab rat, Michael." She couldn't help the hurt that crept into her tone. The anger had been surprisingly short-lived.

On the other end of the comm, Michael straightened abruptly. "That wasn't my intention, Leah. I'm sorry. I know very well what a lab rat feels like and I didn't mean to do that to you." His eyes narrowed and she looked away, wishing she could just end the comm and crawl under her bed to hide for a few centuries. "Look, can we start over? It was foolish of me not to realize-"

She'd never heard Michael Amber so contrite. This was a man used to giving orders and not taking any guff from anyone. That he was sincerely sorry, she saw immediately.

"All right," she said softly. She raised her eyes to meet his across the screen. "What time do you want me and where?" His gaze sparked and she realized the double entendre in her innocent words. She laughed.

Just like that the tension between them broke and they were back on easier footing.

"Forget I said that," she joked.

"Never." Michael's voice growled across the comm. "But for dinner, I'd like you at my quarters in half a standard. Wear civilian clothes. A dress of some kind, if you have one handy, and leave off the underwear."

"Michael!" She was scandalized. "I didn't agree to anything other than talking tonight."

"But you're going to have my baby, Leah." His voice deepened as his eyes burned into hers through the screen. "We'll talk about it, sure. But then we'll act on it. I'm a Dom, sweetheart. You knew that. Now you need to learn what that really means. Leave off the panties and wear your hair down. It's a small enough request."

He cut the comm, leaving her muttering. "Damn you, Michael Amber." She stalked toward her closet to dig out a dress. She didn't wear them often, but she still had a few from the old days, when she'd been a newlywed woman embarking on a happy life, not a career soldier living on a space station.

Things had changed drastically when her husband-and most other men-had died. She'd taken up arms and joined the military, taking the place of the many men in her family and tribe who'd defended humanity in centuries past. She'd never seriously thought of the military as a career, but found she liked the order and discipline.

The Blackfoot tribe had been cut in half, but her grandmother had been Leah's inspiration. General Adelaide Blackfoot was too old to serve now, but she helped guide the tribe as a member of the Council of Elders and kept tabs on her granddaughter, following Leah's career from afar. Leah looked forward to the letters and comms her grandmother sent every standard month or so. She wasn't the only Blackfoot woman serving in the military now, but she was the highest ranked and the closest relation to the old general. Leah liked carrying on the tradition of service. She also liked the idea she was helping protect what was left of the human worlds after the plague had nearly destroyed them all.

Then there was Michael.

She loved working with him. His decisive nature reminded her of her lost family members. In that way, at least, he was very much like her father and brothers had been. He didn't wait to gather consensus. He saw his way forward and acted on his decisions. He wasn't foolish or rash, but he was definitely a leader, not a follower. She liked that. Perhaps more than she should, considering they worked so closely together.

Tonight would take that working relationship and change it forever. Tonight she would see him as a woman sees a man, not as a subordinate views a superior officer. She was looking forward to it, but at the same time, she was scared to death.

Deciding to put it out of her mind for the moment, she chose a short, cobalt blue dress and dressed for dinner. At the last moment, she decided to leave off the underwear, feeling scandalously decadent as she walked down the corridor toward Michael's private quarters. Luckily, she didn't pass anyone in the hall. This area of the station was restricted to the highest ranks and contained only private quarters, so the chances of running into anyone at all weren't high.

Before she could chicken out, she pushed the chime. A moment later, the door slid open and Michael's voice came to her from the dimly lit interior of his living room.

"Come in, Leah." She entered hesitantly, unable to see well for a moment as her eyes adjusted from the brightly lit corridor to the dusky twilight inside. "Close and lock," Michael commanded the computer that regulated the door. She heard the panel slide shut, and then click into secure mode. They were locked in until Michael's voice command released them.

As her eyes adjusted, she noted candles burning on a small table set for two. Michael sat just behind the candles on the far end of the room, watching her.

"I'm glad you're here, Leah." He glanced at his wrist chrono. "On time, too."

She squared her chin, refusing to be unsettled by his burning stare. "I told you I'd be here and here I am."

He stood and skirted the table, walking toward her. She held her ground, unwilling to be intimidated by his almost predatory walk. Their eyes met and held as he drew near.

"I've always admired that about you, Leah. You're a woman of your word." He stopped just a foot away, his fingers tracing over her cheek as gentle as a butterfly's wings. "Your beautiful hair is loose." His palm opened to caress the back of her head and down her back. "So then, I can assume you've followed my instructions to the letter?"

His hand slid lower over her ribs, into the curve of her waist, and then down over her ass. He squeezed, making her gasp.

"No panty lines." His smile was downright wicked. "Good girl, Leah."

"I could be wearing a thong." Some devil of mischief made her want to tease him. His eyes sparkled with challenge as his lips curved upward and his hand roamed even lower, dragging up the short skirt of her soft blue dress.

"You like to live dangerously, don't you?" He pulled her closer, his other hand working at raising her skirt now as he grinned. "If you disobeyed me, you know I'll have to punish you, don't you? Or is that what you're hoping for?"

She gasped as his hot palms found the skin of her naked ass. He cupped her, stroking in a circular motion as he pulled her hard up against him. His cock burned her, a hot, long length pressing into the swell of her belly.

His fingers moved then, as his gaze held hers, sweeping inward as he sought the dark crevice between her cheeks. At the first touch of his blunt fingers, she started, but he gentled her, drawing her closer as he swept his hand downward, trailing the crack of her ass provocatively.

"I don't feel a thong, but maybe I should inspect a little more closely."

His devil's grin teased her as he lifted her clear off her feet. She wasn't a small woman, but the easy way Michael picked her up and carried her around made her feel downright delicate. He walked her backwards, toward the overstuffed couch and lay her down upon it.

"Michael, I-" She placed one palm against his muscular chest, but he stilled her objections with a light kiss.

Before she knew it, she was on her back on the wide couch, Michael's hard body pressing her in to the soft cushions. His mouth searched hers, driving her temperature higher and hotter. At length he broke away, his hands were under her skirt. In fact, the dress had been lifted clear up to her waist, exposing her lower body to rub against the soft fabric of Michael's black trousers.

"I meant to take this slow, but I can't Leah. I

want you too much."

The look in his eyes stilled her objections. She read real need there. Need for her.

Touching his face, she reached up and kissed him lightly. "Don't wait, Michael. We can talk later."

He groaned, but his eyes were torn. She knew every look, every nuance of his expression. She'd read them all over the past years of working with him. She understood his desire now, caught between having her and giving her the words he thought she wanted to hear.

She stroked his beloved face again. "Make love to me now, Michael. I don't want to wait anymore." She took a breath for courage. "I've been dreaming of what it would be like for too long."

"You, too?" A spark lit his eyes. "I thought it was just me, wondering how I would fit inside you, how you would scream when I made you come. I want to know, Leah. I've wanted to know for more than two years."

Her womb clenched as she read the truth of his words in his expression. To think, he'd wanted her too. It was a heady thought.

"I'm going to make this so good for you," he promised, kissing his way down her throat, over her breasts, still covered in fabric, and down to her bare waist. Stopping there for a moment, he leaned back, hovering over her as he looked downward. She'd groomed for him, trimming the curling hair she liked to keep short for comfort.

Once upon a time, she'd shaved there all the time, but for the past few years, she hadn't gone to that much trouble. She hadn't been entirely sure where this night would end, but she'd wanted to be prepared. Still, she hadn't counted on jumping him the moment she walked in the door. Yet she had a good idea where her provocative words would lead and still, she'd uttered them.

"I like the look of your pussy, Leah. Neat and orderly, just like you." He grinned up at her. "It'll be my pleasure to corrupt you."

She laughed as he moved lower, his warm hands settling on her thighs. She hadn't had a man since before her husband took ill with the jit virus. It had been years, but her body knew what it wanted-or rather *who* it wanted. She felt her cream flow, dampening the insides of her thighs as Michael's powerful hands spread her legs apart.

Rough fingers stroked through the slickness, parting her outer lips as his eyes devoured her. She felt utterly exposed and yet completely safe and protected. Michael had that way about him. His eyes practically glowed as he learned the shape of her. His fingers delved deeper, circling her clit and making her squirm before diving into her darkness.

His eyes held hers as two long fingers learned the depth and breadth of her passage. The expression on his face was one she would never forget. She felt stunned, feeling even this small part of him within her for the first time. It had been so long, and never had she been touched with such decisive, knowledgeable hands. It was true, she was learning, that the Sons of Amber more than knew their way around a woman's body. At least Michael did, and she was loving every minute of it.

"Do you like that?" His voice tempted her.

"You know I do." It was an effort to speak, but she managed it, barely.

He grinned at her, adding another finger to the two already stretching her. "I'm going to love planting my baby in you, Leah. I've never felt so strongly about a woman before. Never wanted one as much as I want you."

She moaned a little as he started to move within her, rubbing that little spot that made her breathless. "You don't...have to...say that, Michael. It's all right."

He stilled.

Her eyes shot open and met his. He looked like a thundercloud, though he seemed just the tiniest bit unsure of himself, which was definitely out of character for him.

"You of all people know I don't say things I don't mean." She nodded, and he rewarded her by moving his fingers gently within her. "I don't understand it myself, Leah, but it's true." He lowered his head and kissed the slight swell of her belly, moving lower. "I want you. More than I've ever wanted any other woman." His words teased her curls, then her clit as he licked out and teased her with his tongue. His hand moved faster as his breath sighed over her most sensitive skin.

When his mouth opened directly over her clit and fastened on, she came harder than she ever had before. Michael rode her through the climax, his hands gentling her as he let her come and come. She'd never climbed so high, so fast, and she didn't come down. Although the climax faded after a while, Michael kept her on a plateau near the summit of her pleasure. He was a master at playing her body and he proved it to her in those long minutes of foreplay while he learned her body and taught her a thing or two about it as well.

By the time he stalked back up her body, she was ready for anything. Except for him to leave her.

Michael stood, his gaze sweeping over her as she lay, exposed-probably like some cheap hooker on the couch. Leah felt her skin heat with embarrassment, but Michael moved, lifting her into his arms as he strode forcefully toward the door at the far end of the room. His bedroom, she guessed.

She hid her face in his neck, loving the smell and feel of him. He was so strong, carrying her around like a kitten, he made her feel small and protected. It was something she hadn't felt since she was a child. Since before the jits attacked so devastatingly.

Michael sat her on the bed, then swept her blue dress up and completely off in one swift movement. He nudged her back onto the wide bed, directing her with a pointed look.

"It's going to be fast this time, Leah. I can't wait anymore."

Reading the urgent look in his eyes, Leah understood. He'd held off to pleasure her, but this time would be for him. She wanted to give him whatever he wanted. Especially after the generous climax he'd given her.

Scooting back on the soft bed, Leah felt no embarrassment as she spread her legs wide. Michael stood to the side, watching her every movement as he stripped cleanly and efficiently. His clothes went flying somewhere behind him as Leah watched.

His chest was a thing of beauty, sculpted

perfection of hard muscles and sinewy strength. His legs were the same. Long, lean and muscular in a way that made her mouth water. But his cock. Now that was a work of art.

Thick, hard and ready, Leah knew Michael would bring her more pleasure than she could ever remember. He was built on the large side, with heavy balls that she knew held a large amount of sperm. He'd been designed that way, so he could play his part in helping repopulate the human worlds.

But all she cared about just then was how he was going to empty those balls into her. Sons of Amber, it was rumored, were always ready. They didn't need much down time because of their superior genetics and they'd even been known to wear a woman out if given half a chance.

Leah, though, had always had a strong sexual appetite. She wondered which of them would give up first. It would be her pleasure to find out.

Licking her lips, Leah sat forward. She wanted to taste that cock, if he'd let her.

Chapter Five

Michael couldn't believe the sex kitten hidden under Leah's starched uniform. When she'd walked into his quarters wearing that sexy blue dress, it was all he could do to speak. Then that daring comment about the thong had teased him beyond reason. He hadn't meant to move quite this fast, but there was no going back now. Leah was a siren and he was glad to take the plunge. He'd die for her. Happily.

He saw her coming toward him, her intent clear, but he was in charge here. Not that he objected to her wanting to touch him. Just not now. Not when he was so close. This woman challenged even his legendary control.

"Lay back, Leah. Spread your legs and show me where you want me."

She pouted for a second, but moved to comply. He liked the way she followed his orders. This wasn't like when they were in the office. Then, she behaved like any other soldier under his command-though she was incredibly intuitive about what he wanted. Often she knew what he wanted before he did himself, which is what made her indispensable as his XO. But this was different. This was a woman-not a soldier-giving over control to her man.

She did it almost unconsciously, as he'd hoped

she would. He got the feeling they'd be compatible this way, judging from their long acquaintance. Leah wasn't anyone's pushover. She was a strong woman with very definite opinions, but she was willing to let him lead here, and that's what counted. They worked together so well because he respected her ability just as she respected his authority. They trusted each other to know and understand what the other could handle.

Michael was gratified to see that carried over. Leah followed his lead, not because she was weak and needed to be led, but because she trusted him. Without that trust, Mike would never have agreed to take this to the next step.

Leah lay back on the bed and did as he asked, pushing her legs wide apart. He licked his lips, marveling at the sight. She held out one hand, beckoning.

"Come to me now, Michael. I need you."

Her voice whispered across his senses. How many times had he dreamed of just such a scene? And here she was, finally, in his bed. He could wait no longer.

Michael knelt on the bed, crawling over her until her much smaller frame was bracketed by him. His cock nestled into her slick folds, his gaze holding hers as he held himself up on his elbows above her. Bending his spine, he bent to kiss her voluptuous breasts. He hadn't paid them nearly as much attention as he wanted, but they had all night. For now, he had to be inside her or he'd go insane.

Pushing as gently as he could manage, he slid into her channel, watching her eyes for any sign of distress. He was big and she was tight, though he didn't sense any discomfort on her part, which was a relief. He pushed further inside, loving the way her lips fell open and her eyes half-closed. Those pretty eyes of hers held him spellbound as he shoved all the way home, resting there for a moment while she caught her breath.

"How are you doing?" He nipped her lips, waiting for a reply.

"I'm good. Oh, God, Michael. It's been a long time."

"It's never been like this before."

She laughed as he lifted up to scan her expression. He read joy there.

"That's what I was going to say."

He leaned back to kiss her face. "It only gets better from here."

Her hands swept over his shoulders and around his neck as she dragged him down. "Show me."

Michael started to move, gently at first, but then with increasing enthusiasm. He was barely holding on to his control, though this was by far the tamest sex he'd engaged in for years. Straight missionary without even a hint of kink. His brothers would never believe it.

Mike had earned a bit of a reputation among his kind for rather inventive bedroom play, but nothing before could compare to this simple pleasure with this special woman. Michael realized it was the woman who made the difference, not any special technique he could dream up. Though he'd love to try a few things with Leah, if she'd let him.

But that was for later. For now, he was nearing

the end of his rope as she came around him. He drove her to the crest again, wanting her to come at least once more before he did. He inserted one hand between them, playing with her clit as she gasped and moaned beneath him. *That's it*, he thought, as he felt the tremble in her limbs, the clutch of her inner muscles around him. She panted as she came again, pulling him along with her.

He erupted within her, bathing her womb in a torrent of his seed. He knew that's what she wanted. She wanted his baby, but he hoped she wanted him, too-at least a little.

He'd never wanted that before, but with Leah, he was learning fast, all bets were off. He'd never wanted to break a woman's heart by having her care for him and then leave her. He'd always done his best to remind the women he bedded that he was not available for anything long-term. Hell, he didn't even do short-term. He did appearances. That was it. One night stands. Then he was gone, never to be seen again. It was best not to encourage those women to care for him. He didn't like hurting them when duty called him away.

But he wanted Leah to care for him. He wanted to have a relationship with her-something he'd never wanted before. He wanted to fuck her over and over, for many nights to come. As long as she'd let him. And he wanted her to want him to do it. Not because she wanted his child, but because she wanted him.

Coming down from the most amazing climax he could ever recall, Michael rolled, clutching her body close to his as he positioned her over him. He stayed within her body, wanting to be part of her for a little longer. That was new, too. This woman was showing him things about himself he'd never seen before and it was heady stuff, as well as a little frightening.

He kissed her shoulder, her neck, the ridges of her ear as he settled her on top of his body like a living blanket. She was sleepy and compliant in his arms, nuzzling into his chest in the most satisfying way.

"I think I'm going to keep you for a while, Leah." He licked her earlobe. "How does the next year sound?"

Drowsy eyes met his as she levered up on one arm to see him. Her expression was adorably confused.

"Do we have that long? I mean, don't you have to...um...service others?"

"As long as you want me, Leah. I'm yours. Nobody forces Sons to take appointments. I'll still make my deposits, but I'll cancel the few appointments on my calendar. I don't want any other woman. Not while I have you."

Her eyes narrowed and he thought he saw hope flare in them before she shook her head, just once. Lowering herself back to lie on his chest, she snuggled into him.

"I won't presume, but I'll take whatever you'll give me, Michael. I've missed this."

"Sex?"

"No. Well, yes. I've missed sex, but mostly," he felt her little fingers tangling in the hair on his chest, "I've missed this closeness. This sharing with a man. It's one of the reasons I love working with you so much. I was used to my family-my father and brothers. I was the only girl and I spent a lot of time with them, and then later, with my husband. We were friends. I missed having that male perspective and when I started working for you, I found that again. I valued your friendship, Michael. I never told you that, but it's true." His arms stroked over her soft skin as he took in her words. She was saying something important here, though he didn't like thinking about all she'd lost. "I loved my husband, but he was never like the other men in my family. He wasn't military, so he didn't understand my roots and he let my father and brothers walk all over him." She laughed softly, but it was a sad sound. He hugged her close. "He wasn't at all like you, Michael. I think-" She kissed his chest, her voice lowering. "I think if I'd known you back then, I would never have married him. God, that's a terrible thing to say."

He held her tight, floored by her admission. "Never fear the truth, Leah. We can't change the past, but we can decide our future. I want us to continue working together and sleeping together. I want you in my office and in my bed. Even after you get pregnant and the baby comes."

"But we were only supposed to be making a baby here."

"I know," he prayed he was right about her feelings. "But I want more. I'm hoping you do to. I'm hoping you want more than just my baby. Am I right in thinking that maybe you want me-at least a little?"

She lifted up and met his eyes. "Oh, Michael. I do want you. I've wanted you for a very long time." She kissed him then and he felt as if he'd been given the world. He felt the truth of her words in her kiss and returned the sentiment. She pulled back far too soon. "I mean," she smiled sheepishly, "I want a baby too, but I've admired you for a long time. If-no, when-you move on, I'll treasure the baby we make together."

His cock hardened again within her and he began to move. "Right now, I can't imagine a time I won't want to be with you, Leah. Let's take it one step at a time. Tonight we'll get a start on that baby, and eventually have some dinner." He grinned at her as she began to move in counterpoint to his thrusts. "Maybe I'll even show you a little bit of what I like in the way of Domination. If that doesn't scare you off, we'll proceed from there." He reached up and bit her neck lightly. "One thing is sure, though, we can never go back."

"No," she leaned up and stroked his hair back from his face, "there's no going back. But I really don't want to."

"Good." Michael lifted her so she sat astride him and put a pillow behind his head so he could view her better. "Then ride me, woman. Do it right and I'll feed you dinner." He winked and growled when she responded by squeezing her inner muscles around his cock.

* * * *

Eventually they ate dinner, but it was a strange affair. Michael hand fed her every bite and demanded she suck his cock between dishes. Leah really didn't mind that at all. Especially when he sat her on the table and declared *she* was desert.

The next morning her nipples were sore from his lips and teeth, her pussy was tender, but her mouth could only grin. She stumbled back to her quarters, which were close by his, early in the morning to shower and change into a uniform. They were going to have to devise some kind of plan if this kept up. She'd almost run into two of her junior officers on her way back and only ducking behind a bulkhead had saved her from speculative looks and being the talk of the station grapevine.

Michael had Dominated her a little last night, though if the rumors she'd heard about some of the bedroom antics he'd gotten up to in the past were to be believed, he'd been very tame indeed. Still, she didn't mind following his orders as much as she thought she would. In fact, there was something incredibly sexy about a man who knew exactly what he wanted and didn't mind telling you how to go about pleasing him.

She worried as she entered her office, wondering how they would interact today after the marathon session last night. They never did get around to talking much about their relationship or how they'd deal with her plan to have Michael's baby. She knew Michael assumed she'd continue working for him even after the baby was born, but she just didn't know if she wanted to do that.

On the one hand, she couldn't stand the idea of leaving Michael. Especially now. She'd resigned herself to quitting when she'd made the decision to be impregnated with his sperm, but now that they'd changed the nature of their relationship and Michael knew about the baby, she didn't think she could go through with that part of her original plan. No, now she was warming to the idea of having Michael know his child and be part of their lives for as long as he could.

She knew she couldn't keep him, but by the same token, she wanted to give him the chance to know his baby. She didn't believe it was fair to ask him to father a baby he would never know. He had a right to be involved in her child's life, if he wanted to. And if his duties allowed.

Thoughts jumbled her mind as she sat down at her desk and began her day. She was habitually the first person in the office. Michael usually came in right after her or sometimes they arrived together and worked companionably in their respective offices until the rest of the staff arrived.

Other parts of the station had control during the main command staff's off-shift and Leah's subordinates officially took Command and Control back an hour after she started her workday. In this way, she got a head start on anything that might've happened during her sleep interval and was ready to deal with it.

Luckily nothing of much import awaited her that morning. She didn't know if she could have dealt with a crisis on top of the nerves churning in her stomach as she prepared to face Michael after their night of passion. She'd left awkwardly this morning, stealing out of his suite while he was in the shower, like a thief in the night. She knew he wouldn't be happy about it, but she'd needed time to think-and clean up-before facing him again.

She heard his deep voice ring through the outer

office as he greeted one of her junior officers who sounded as if she was just arriving herself. The floorplan was set up so that her office was the buffer between Michael's and the bustling C and C. Anyone wanting to get to the Commandant had to go through her first and she had enough rank and authority to deal with most matters without having to bother Michael for every little thing.

She had an assistant who sat just outside her door and acted as a further level of screening, also keeping a constant eye on the goings on in C and C, ready to call her if needed. In addition, both Leah and Michael had heads up displays they could monitor to keep track of operations throughout the sector. C and C was the gathering point for information and both Leah and Michael had stations there when needed, but preferred to spend a good portion of their day-barring a crisis-in the quiet of their offices, away from the bustle .

Leah gathered her wits, trying to be as nonchalant as possible when Michael strode in and shut her door behind him. She knew from long experience that once the door was sealed, the office was sound tight. No one would hear anything they said, which was both a blessing and a curse at the moment.

Michael walked right up to her, not stopping until he'd taken her in his arms and kissed her to within an inch of her life. Her senses spun her mind overloaded, and all she could think of was the feel of his lips on hers, the flavor of him, the strength in his hands holding her tight against his powerful body.

When he drew back, she was dazed.

"Good morning, Leah." His voice was a husky whisper.

"Good morning, Michael."

"Now that's the way I wanted to start my day. Instead, I came out of the shower to an empty room. Why'd you sneak out?"

She could see the disapproval in his eyes. "I..." What could she say that wouldn't make her sound foolish? "I needed some time alone. To think."

"All right," he let go and set her away, stepping back. "Did it help?" His gaze studied her.

"To be honest, not really."

"I know you wanted to talk last night, but the situation got out of control fast. How about we try again tonight? Bring a change of clothes with you this time and maybe we can shower together tomorrow morning. Start the day off right. And maybe this time we'll actually get to talk a bit before the fireworks begin. What do you say?"

Relieved, she nodded. "I'd like that."

"Good." His smile warmed her as he moved away, heading for his office door. "Now, what have we got on the agenda for today. Lunch with Admiral Watts, right? I'll need those force reduction figures and redeployment schedule. And I don't care what the Admiral's staff says, I want you at that table with me. No way am I going to sit through another one of her poorly veiled innuendoes or blatant attempts at seduction. With you there, she'll think twice before putting her foot in it again."

She laughed. "Poor Commandant. All his subordinates want to seduce him."

"Maybe so," he winked at her. "But you're the

only one I'll actually let do it."

She knew everything would be all right then. Michael was in a great mood and it carried over to everything they did that day and for the days after. Each night they dined together and she stayed over, being careful not to be seen. They made love long into the night and woke together in Michael's big bed the next day, starting it together before they headed for work. Together.

They never did manage to talk all that much. They were always too hungry for each other by the time they were alone at night. It didn't seem to matter much until those times when Leah thought about the future. Then she'd worry until Michael caught her eye and winked. He had to know there was something preying on her mind and he probably had a good idea of what it was, but neither of them had the strength to resist the other long enough to discuss the nitty gritty of what would happen in the future.

Three, then four days passed, and they fell into a routine of sorts, until one morning they arrived at work to find a report from Tyron. Michael took it into his office and closed the door. An hour later, an urgent transmission came through and she entered the office, knowing this was important enough to interrupt whatever he was doing.

Chapter Six

"Ty is on tight beam."

Leah's voice caressed him as she bustled into Michael's office, all business. She came around his desk and flicked on the controls that would bring the highly irregular signal to his comm unit. If Ty were contacting them this way, something was definitely up. His brother's face came up on the unit, a bit grainy, but Mike could read the urgency in Ty's eyes.

"Brother, things are worse than we suspected. Someone very highly placed is collaborating with the jits, allowing them to capture and transport human women and turning a blind eye as long as the jits pay up. Mike, someone is selling human females to the jit pirates." Mike's fist hit the desk as anger rode him. "Look, I don't have enough proof to nail anyone yet, and I think I'm close to finding out who's behind this, but my cover is a bit precarious. I may need more help here, Mike. Send a brother."

"Dammit! I'll come myself. This is too serious." Mike sent back the immediate, furious reply, knowing he'd have to wait the few moments it took for the tight beam signal to reach Ty. He turned to Leah. "What've we got in that region? Can we use a legitimate trip out there to cover our real purpose?"

"There's Smithson. She's got jurisdiction. We

could always do an inspection tour and it wouldn't raise many eyebrows after her latest snafu."

"Good thinking." Damn, he loved this woman's quick mind and capable intellect. "Set the wheels in motion, Leah, but I want you to stay here."

"Like hell."

"Leah, I don't want to put you in danger. If Smithson or one of her people is in on this plot, they may try something."

"All the more reason for me to come along and watch your back. They'll be gunning for you, if anyone. Not me, Michael. You know that's the truth. And I can talk to the other women. They won't talk freely to you, but they'll do so around me."

He hated that she was right.

"If I allow this, we'll have to be all business once we hit Smithson's domain. I don't want her to know I've broken my famous rule for you, Leah." He stood and reached out to stroke her hair back from her face. "Smithson already hates me, and all my staff by association. If she makes a move against me I don't want to give her any added reason to target you specifically."

"Do you really expect she'll make a grab for power? I don't think she has the nerve."

"She acts stupid, but I'm convinced it's all an act. That woman has ambition and I'm the one standing in her way. If she sees an opportunity to discredit me or take me out completely, she'll take it."

Leah came to him, hugging him close. Mike was astounded and very moved that she would show such open affection. It was one of the few times in his life a woman had sought to comfort him, to hug him in reassurance with nothing sexual about it. It was beautiful. No, *she* was beautiful. This woman was so incredibly special.

"Then we won't give her an opportunity, Michael." She snuggled her head into his chest as if it belonged there. Mike brought his hand up and stroked her hair, her back, emotion crowding his senses along with her delicate fragrance. "That woman is a viper."

"I couldn't agree more."

Mike just held her for long moments, enjoying the sensation of her in his arms. He'd never forget this moment.

* * * *

A day and a half later, they were underway. The trip was relatively short, though Mike didn't like being out of touch with Ty while he was undercover. Who knew what the crazy Risker would get in to?

They arrived with little fanfare, an unannounced inspection tour taking Smithson and her entire staff by surprise. Just the way he wanted it.

They were given the best suite the small station had to offer and Mike installed Leah in one of the two bedrooms. He knew they were under surveillance, so he kept Leah close, but not too close. He wouldn't put Leah in even more danger should this mission go wrong by letting Smithson know just how deeply they were involved personally.

When Mike switched on the jamming devices he did it in private, smiling sinisterly at Smithson's badly hidden cameras in the moment before killing them all with the pulse of interfering frequencies. She had to know now that he was on to her surveillance. It was a dare of a kind, but he didn't expect her to do much about it, and Mike needed the privacy to contact Ty.

"Brother?" Michael was careful of his wording lest others somehow tap into the secure signal.

"What took you so long, Mikel?" Ty's use of the slightly different name alerted Mike to the fact that Ty thought others might be listening. It also spoke of just whom he thought could be monitoring the conversation. Jits, no doubt. The crazy Risker had gone deep undercover and was probably up to his ears in pirates.

"You know how it is. When can we meet up?"

"I'm with some friends right now. How about I comm back when I know what my schedule will be like? Say in about two standards?"

"I'll be here. Don't be late."

"Wouldn't dream of it. Take care, brother."

Leah was with Michael two standards later when his secure comm beeped. Michael turned on the jamming device and answered promptly.

"Can't talk long, Mike," Ty's voice came urgently over the unit. "Meet me at the following coordinates in exactly three standards. Don't be late." A string of coordinates lit the screen of Michael's secure wrist comp.

"I'll be there." He signed off and turned to face Leah's determined expression.

"I'm coming, too. You can't go out there without anyone to watch your back."

"Leah, be reasonable. Most likely Ty's infiltrated

the pirate network I bet is running in the background of this station. That's no place for a woman, even one as capable as yourself."

"Thanks. I think. But the fact remains. You can't go in there alone. What if it's a trap?"

"What if it is? Do you think you'll fare any better with jit pirates than I will? They'll have you naked and spread before you can say hello." He recognized that stubborn set to her chin. Mike sighed, knowing she would follow whether he allowed it or not. Some Dom he was turning out to be. This woman always seemed to get her way. He could deny her nothing. "Dammit, Leah! If you do this, you'll do it by my rules. Do you understand?"

"Yes, sir."

"Oh, so now you want to play obedient little soldier." He had to chuckle at the mischief in her eyes. "I'll remember this, sweetheart. Believe it. Now, if you go, you go as a civilian. You'll leave behind all identification. Do you have anything sexy to wear?"

* * * *

Leah had packed a few pieces for casual wear, and with a few adjustments and some quick thinking, she had a reasonably nice outfit in her carryall as they sneaked out of the visiting officers' quarters later that night. They'd go in uniform until they hit a station hotel, then go in separately to use the facilities and stash their uniforms in the room she'd rent on her altered civilian ID chip. They'd rendezvous in the hall and work their way to the more deserted parts of the station-the mechanical sections-where they'd meet with Tyron.

Everything went as planned. The hotel was as nondescript as possible, with no live staff. Everything was handled by computer and the rooms were incredibly small, but suitable for their purposes. No one would remark on a male human entering or exiting because no one was around to see.

It was off-shift so most of the station was either sleeping or on duty at their various posts. Few, if any, saw them in the halls as they made their way stealthily forward. When they reached the coordinates Ty had given, Mike pulled Leah close to his side. She trusted his enhanced senses to ferret out threats her regular human ears couldn't hear. She knew Sons were gifted with superior genetics that made them smarter, faster, and sharper than regular humans.

"Long time, no see, brother." Ty's voice came to them from just ahead as the man stepped into the bare light of the poorly lit hall.

"Good to see you too, Ty. How goes it?" Michael was being cautious, Leah sensed, feeling the tension in the arm wrapped possessively around her waist.

"I see you've got a new toy." Ty nodded in her direction. She wanted to be appalled by the phrasing, but she sensed more was being said here than met the eye. Ty knew full well who and what she was. She didn't look *that* different in civilian clothing. He had to recognize her, yet he was acting as if she were a stranger. That meant they were being watched. She played along, knowing the men were posing as jit'suku pirates.

They could do it, too. Where regular human

males didn't usually grow to the size of jit'suku males, Sons of Amber were as large, hard muscled, and every bit as fierce as the alien warriors. Sons could easily pass as jits and it was rumored some jit DNA was actually used in their design, which was probably a big part of what made them immune to the jit virus.

But if they were posing as jits, what was she? Girlfriend? Not likely. She was probably relegated to the role of sex slave. She would have objected, but being Michael's sex slave held a certain amount of forbidden appeal, and they really needed to get more information in order to break up this smuggling ring.

"I'm still training her." Michael let her go. "Turn around, Lilla. Show my brother your perky ass."

She gasped at his command, something inside her squirming to heated life. Slowly, she turned, uncertain at first, following the silent direction of his spinning finger, indicating he wanted her to twirl slowly. He stopped her the same way, shocking her when he reached out and grabbed her ass with a firm hand, squeezing snuggly as she rose on her toes.

"Take a look at that." Michael's voice was admiring as he acted out a very frank and tactile appraisal of her posterior. Warmth flooded her womb as his fingers caressed down her crack.

"Nice piece," Ty said, patting her other cheek familiarly as she gasped. When she looked over her shoulder at him, he winked with that devilish smile he was famous for. Women sighed over Tyron's smile. Little did Leah ever imagine he'd be fondling her tush in a public corridor in front of Michael and whoever else might be watching, and even more, that she'd like it. "So what brings you here, brother?"

Just that easily, she was dismissed. She kept silent, walking behind Michael as he'd instructed her to do when he went over the exhaustive list of possible scenarios before they ever left his quarters. He'd prepared her for all contingencies and though this was one of the less likely occurrences, she was ready to act the slave-as long as that's all it was…an act.

"I'm looking for a few more like her. I've got a buyer lined up who can take at least fifty if I can get my hands on them."

"Fifty?" Ty whistled as they walked. "That's more than you've ever handled on your own before."

"I know. That's why I came looking for you, Ty. I'll cut you in for half if you'll help me."

Ty made a show of considering his offer. "I don't know, Mik. I'm working for someone else now and he's got a sweet deal here."

Michael made a show of looking around. "Yeah, I was kind of surprised when your coordinates led me to a human military station. You've got brass balls, brother, or friends in very high places."

Ty held up his hands, palms outward though he smiled craftily. "Not my friends, Mik. Like I said, I'm working for someone else now. He's the one with the connections."

Michael tilted his head, as if considering. "You think he might be up for the job then? I still need to come up with fifty women pretty quick."

"I'm not sure, but I'll introduce you. You can ask him yourself."

They'd stopped in front of a small hatch and Ty

motioned them inside as he opened the door. It was a small bedroom, undoubtedly with surveillance. *Perhaps*, she thought, *the jit leader wants to see if we're on the level.* They'd have to put on a bit of a show, but she was willing to trust Michael to know her boundaries. Though she was fast discovering where Michael Amber was concerned, she had precious few.

"What's this? Can't we talk to him now? I'm in a hurry to get this job completed, Ty."

Ty smiled and stepped back. "It's off-shift. Nothing goes on here during these hours. Rest, sleep, whatever you like. I'll see if I can arrange a meeting for early next shift. Until then, stay here. I'm going to lock you in, Mik. It's for your own safety. As you said, we are on a human military station, after all."

"I don't like this, brother." A hint of steel entered Michael's voice as he held the door open with one hand as Ty stepped through back into the hall.

"Trust me, Mik. This is the way it has to be."

Michael sighed and stepped back, allowing Tyron to close and lock the door from the outside.

Then he turned to her.

Chapter Seven

"Strip."

Mike liked the way her eyes flared at his order. She was playing the submissive now, and he loved the rush of power he felt at her willing acquiescence. She'd been with him every step of the way on their journey of sexual discovery so far, but now he'd have to push her farther than he'd ever pushed her before. Their very lives depended on it.

Ty had gotten them into something much more dangerous than Mike had bargained for when he'd let Leah to follow him into the bowels of the station. If he'd known they'd end up going undercover with jit pirates right here, Mike would never have let Leah out of the cabin. He'd have tied her up, if necessary, but he wouldn't have allowed her within a light year of this kind of danger.

There was no law in this part of the station. He knew Smithson-or someone equally high ranking-had to be in on this in order for a population of male pirates to have taken over this much of the predominantly female-run station. Something very strange was going on here and Mike vowed to get to the bottom of it. One way or another.

But right now he had a little show to put on for the cameras undoubtedly watching his every move.

He hoped Leah realized it too, but judging from the way she followed his lead, she knew something was up. Good. That would make this easier.

"I said, strip, slave." He moved around her, waiting just a moment before reaching up and ripping off her tunic, reducing it to shreds. She cried out and he smacked her ass once as a reminder. She quieted beautifully. "You disappoint me, woman. When I give a command, I expect you to obey immediately. Is that clear?"

"Yes."

"Yes, what?" She hesitated and he tugged her head back, yanking her hair gently. "Who is your master, little one?"

"You are." Her voice washed over his senses, sending him into orbit with an arousal the likes of which even he had never before experienced. Having Leah at his full command was a new and very exciting experience.

"Very good. Now what do you call me?"

"Master." Her whisper floated to his ear, pleasing him greatly.

"Good girl." He patted her ass, caressing the soft skin almost absently, though he would never forget anything about this moment if he lived forever. "Now get on the bed and spread your legs. Show me your pussy."

He stood at the foot of the bed as she scrambled onto the platform, obeying him with grace and speed. She seemed eager to please him, causing his cock to jerk under his clothing. Quickly, he stripped out of his nondescript flight suit and grasped his cock in one hand. It was fairly screaming for release.

"Rub yourself, kitten. Make yourself wet and ready for me." From what he could see, she was already quite wet, which worked to his advantage. He didn't think he could hold back much this first time. He wanted her too badly.

No, this first time would be hard and fast. He'd waited too long. He needed her now. In the back of his mind he also knew the watchers would expect little in the way of care be shown to a slave girl. They expected him to be just like them-taking what he wanted brutally with little regard for the human woman the jits considered inferior.

It might look brutal to those who watched, but Mike would make sure Leah enjoyed every minute of his domination, his desire...his loving. Because that's what it felt like, though he'd never really experienced such a thing before. He felt things deep in his soul for this woman. If it wasn't love, it was something very close.

Mike knelt on the bed, throwing the rest of his clothing to the floor negligently as he crawled between Leah's spread thighs. She was wet and glistening, her abdomen palpitating as she neared a peak. And he hadn't even touched her yet. She was eager for him...for his dominance.

"Hands up, woman. Above your head and don't move them. This is going to be hard and fast. Just the way I like it."

He winked at her as he came over her body, leaning on his hands as he bent down to kiss her nipples, sucking them deep, one at a time. She moaned and writhed enticingly beneath him as he seated his cock at her dripping entrance. He rubbed his length against her, up and down her slot as she moaned again.

"Please," she begged. It was music to his ears. "Please, Master!"

Unable to hold back another minute, Mike reared back and plunged his cock home within her tight sheath. She cried out at the sudden entrance, but he could feel her with him every step of the way. She climaxed as he pumped just once, deep inside.

"Hang on, sweetheart," he whispered in her ear as he gathered her hips in his hands, preparing for the ride yet to come. When her contractions slowed, he began thrusting. Slow at first, he built his strokes, angling this way and that, loving the feel of her gloving him in warmth. She was built for him. For this. He'd never had any other woman feel so right.

Mike fucked in and out of her tight pussy, reveling in the feel of her, the little sounds she made as she rose higher in passion once more. She was so responsive to him. Even playing the role of slave. She was like a dream. The perfect woman to match his Dominant nature.

He'd never dared push her this far when they were together. He'd tempered his dominance so as not to scare her off, but circumstances had played right into this. Michael had to act the role of master here, fulfilling some of his baser-and very real-needs at the same time. He thrilled inside every time Leah called him master. He'd heard the word from many other women, but never one he admired this much. Never one he knew whose will was as strong, if not stronger, than his own. Never had it felt so damn good to know the woman he fucked surrendered to him utterly, and by surrendering, captured him completely.

Michael shoved into her a few more times, pushing her, sensing her nearing a peak. This time, he went over with her, shooting his load within her hot depths. She cried out, but he captured her words with his mouth, kissing her deeply as he groaned his own completion.

Damn, the woman made him hot. Each time with her was better than the last.

He withdrew, gazing down at her with a feeling of satisfaction. Her eyes were dazed, her body covered with a fine sheen of perspiration that made her sultry skin sparkle. She was magnificent.

He hadn't been able to fuck her on their trip out and going without was difficult. Michael stood from the bed, holding his cock to hide the instant hardening as much as he could. Let the watchers think he had to work to get himself hard again-as they probably would have to do. He needed more of Leah, but he also needed to keep his head. They were no doubt being observed. He had to behave as a jit would. Not as a Son of Amber, who had recuperative powers greater than any other humanoid male.

"Come here, woman, and suck my cock."

Leah's eyes widened, but she moved to comply, playing her role to the hilt. Michael knew her well enough to see the little spark of excitement in her eyes as she sat on the edge of the bed before him. But it wasn't a submissive enough pose for the cameras. Michael stopped her, grabbing a pillow from the bed and tossing it at his feet.

"Kneel."

She blinked up at him only once before complying beautifully. If he wasn't much mistaken, she was enjoying this every bit as much as he was. She actually liked following his orders-even when they were issued roughly. Perhaps even more so.

Michael watched her reactions carefully, cataloging her likes and dislike for future reference. So far, she was with him. More than with him. She seemed eager to know what he'd order her to do next. Hell, she'd even liked it when Ty was palming her ass at his suggestion. He wondered idly if she'd have enjoyed Ty's attentions even if he wasn't around, but decided against it. For one thing, Ty had tried his moves on her a few times over the years when he'd come to see Michael and been shot down every time. Leah was nobody's fool. She liked Ty as a friend, but not as a potential lover. It was Michael's sperm she'd chosen, after all, to make her baby, and Michael's bed she'd been sleeping in for the past weeks.

Her little hand took over from his as she licked the head of his cock. She was very good at giving head and Mike planned to enjoy every moment of it-audience or no. Still, his thoughts raced.

"Did you like my brother, little one? Did you enjoy his touch?"

Wide eyes stared up at him as her movements slowed. He heard a smacking sound as she drew away.

"He's nice, Master," she said softly, "but he isn't you."

Mike's cock twitched in her hands. How did the woman know exactly what to say to send his temperature soaring even higher? She was a mind reader of some kind. Had to be.

"Did I say you could stop?"

"Sorry, Master." She smiled at him before resuming her duties, taking him deep into her throat the way she knew he loved. She was very talented and it wasn't long before he came down her throat, some of his cum spilling out to drip down her flushed cheeks.

When he could stand without swaying, he cupped her cheeks with his palms, wiping away the excess. There was so much he wanted to say but couldn't. Not with the jits watching their every move. He hoped she knew how much she meant to him.

If he'd known they'd be in the thick of things, he never would have taken her with him on this mission. He knew she was a skilled officer who could more than take care of herself, but he hated to see her in danger. It went against his grain to put her in peril, especially now that they were lovers. Even before they'd become intimate, Leah had held a special place in his life. He would send himself and others into the field, keeping her in relative safety on the station, unwilling to risk her more than necessary. She was his anchor and he didn't know what he'd do if anything happened to her.

"Under the covers with you, girl." He couldn't help the affectionate tone in his voice anymore than he could help the gentle way he touched her. He only hoped it didn't look or sound too suspicious to their watchers.

She scrambled into the bed, holding up the corner of the spread for him as he followed. When he tugged her into his arms, she went willingly, snuggling into him as if she belonged there.

They slept for a while, but Michael kept alert for any possible threat. Sons didn't require as much sleep as regular humans, but he put up the pretense of sleep to fit in. Leah slept deeply, secure in his arms. He loved the way she felt there and he spent much of his energy trying to stop thinking about her and focus on the mission. It was difficult, to say the least.

But when the hatch unlocked and slid open, Michael was instantly alert. He didn't move until he recognized Ty's grinning face in the doorway.

"Come on, Mik. You've been invited to dinner." Ty stepped in and threw his pants at him. Michael caught them reflexively as Leah stirred and woke next to him.

Ty looked at the sheet she clutched to her chest and then up to Michael, winking. Son of a bitch, the man was going to get a show, and he knew it. Michael's gut clenched, knowing there was no way to protect Leah's modesty in such a situation. The false expression on Ty's face was enough to tell him they were still being monitored closely.

"Up, girl. We're going to dinner." Michael ripped the covers away and slapped Leah's pretty ass.

Ty whistled between his teeth as he stared at Leah's bouncing tits. She had bigger breasts than anyone had guessed hidden under that uniform, and Michael well knew his brother's preferences. Ty got an eyeful as Michael dressed, then threw Leah's clothing at her. She squirmed into it, Ty watching all the while and enjoying the show, judging by the tightening fit of his pants.

But Michael couldn't object. Neither could Leah, but one look at her flushed face told Michael she enjoyed this a little more than he'd expected. Rather than shame, he read titillation in her eyes-and her perky nipples. They were pushing against the soft fabric of her dress as she smoothed it down. The thin material did nothing to hide her rather obvious excitement.

Michael did his best not to notice the way Ty looked at Leah. It was all part of the act, after all, though Michael knew his brother was duly impressed with Leah's...attributes. They exited the room and Ty led them down several small corridors to a much larger room. Men's voices could be heard and as they entered, Michael counted about fourteen pirates, already seated, eating. There were three tables-one large one in the center and two smaller, flanking it. At the largest table sat what Mike assumed to be the leader of this ragtag group. He had a girl on each knee and one on the floor between his legs.

Ty brought Michael to the chair opposite the leader and introduced them. There were a few tense moments before the jit man nodded and motioned them all to sit and then dinner was served.

A group of women brought the food out and then stayed with the men, to serve it and eat themselves. Some were treated as equals, most as slaves. Michael took his cue from those around him, issuing instructions for Leah as the food was placed before him. She sat on his knee and cut up the meat, serving him first, then herself at his direction.

So far so good.

Everything rolled along fine until the food was gone. Then some of the pirates began desert, but it wasn't sweet rolls they were after.

"So, Mik," the pirate leader leered at Leah, "you want more like her?"

"If at all possible," Michael answered neutrally. He didn't like the look in the man's eyes as he watched Leah.

"Well, let's have a look at her." Some of the other pirates cheered at their leader's words. "Got to know what we're aiming for, don't we?"

Michael felt Leah tense on his knee and her eyes widened with just a hint of fright. Michael tried to sooth her, running his hand over her thigh and squeezing gently where no one could see.

With a little shove, he pushed her off his knee to a standing position between himself and Ty. He could use his brother's help here and knew Leah trusted them both to see to her safety. The next few minutes could get interesting, depending on how these heathen pirates reacted to what he had in mind. Mike had a plan. It was daring, but it might just work to protect Leah and their cover all at the same time.

"Take off your dress, Lil, and show them your tits."

Her eyes widened, but he couldn't back down. This was too important.

Chapter Eight

"Drop the dress, Lilla."

Michael's voice sounded loud to her in the room full of watching pirates. She couldn't believe what he'd just ordered her to do. Yet, she didn't see any way out of this situation. They were badly outnumbered. She had to trust him and hope he had a workable plan.

Her gaze shot to Ty, seated next to Michael at the table. Ty watched her with amused speculation. Only she saw the little wink of reassurance. These two men would look after her as much as possible in this crazy situation. She knew Michael would protect her with his life, but having Ty there as backup-and to stabilize Michael's volatile temper-made her feel just the tiniest bit better, and somewhat disloyal at the same time.

Michael was a Dom. He couldn't help the temper, but Ty didn't suffer from the same affliction. As a Risker, he was always aware of the odds of any given situation and his judgment would be invaluable in this amazingly tense situation.

Still, she hesitated. She was completely naked beneath the dress. She clutched the edges of the neckline as the pirates laughed uproariously.

"Can't control your woman yet, eh, Mik?" One of

the jits leered at her. "Give her time. She'll learn who is master. Of course, I'd be more than happy to help you teach her that lesson."

"Thank you, friend," Michael's voice was smooth, but held recognizable threat. "This wench is mine to teach and I will do so." He snapped at her. "Lilla, come here."

Hesitantly, she shuffled her bare feet to stand even closer to his side. His face was so hard, she barely recognized him under the facade he had to put on in front of these hard alien men. All but his eyes. She could see his desire when he turned his eyes to hers.

His hands moved up to hers, grasping the dress and tearing it down the middle with one powerful tug as the jit pirates cheered lewdly. As she gasped, he slid the remnants down her arms, leaving her completely bare in front of all those men.

"When I give an order, I expect it to be followed without question or demur, Lilla." Michael's eyes bore into hers, lighting a fire in the pit of her womb that shouldn't be. Not here. Not in front of all these people. "You have earned punishment for your failure to comply. Don't make it any worse. Do as I say now and I will wait to punish you until we are in private. Any further disobedience and I will punish you right here and now. Do you understand?"

Slowly she nodded.

"Speak when I ask you a question, Lilla. Do you understand?"

"Yes...Master." Her pussy grew warm as she felt the multitude of eyes on her bare body, but most of all, the expression in Michael's eyes made her want to submit in a way she'd never felt before.

"Good girl." Michael caressed one nipple, tugging at the point and raising a flush of heat to her skin. "Now go sit on the table in front of Ty and show him your pussy."

She jumped, her gaze shooting to the other Son of Amber as he grinned back at her lasciviously. She trusted Michael implicitly, but this...this was a bit much. Michael's hand smacked her ass, bringing her attention back to him sharply.

"I gave an order, missy. Do you wish to disobey?"

"No, Master, but-"

Michael sat back, shaking his head. Disappointment shown on his features, but she could also see something like satisfaction sparkling in his eyes. The men in the room watched too, eager to see how the newcomer would handle his woman.

"Without demur, I said. You've disobeyed me again, woman." Faster than she could blink, Michael had her over his knee. Her bare ass faced Ty and the rest of the men on that side of the room as Michael ran his palm over her cheeks. "You've earned punishment and I warned you it would be public this time, Lilla. Do you understand me, woman?"

"Yes, Master." Her breath came in short pants as her head hung down over Michael's thickly muscled legs.

He smacked her hard, soothing between the open-palmed slaps with circular rubbing motions. He alternated cheeks, hard hits with softer ones, then when she thought this couldn't get any more embarrassing-or arousing-he cavalierly spread her thighs apart and delved into the wetness gathered there with strong, knowing fingers.

"Look at this brother," he talked over her head to Ty and a moment later she felt other fingers probing her cunt. Ty stuck two fingers right up her pussy, stroking deep and rubbing that secret place within her channel that brought her the greatest pleasure. She tried to bite back a moan, but wasn't entirely successful.

"The wench likes her discipline, Mikel. You're a lucky bastard. And her pussy's tight as a drum."

"These human wenches don't see a lot of action with all their males gone. I've had quite a few cute little virgins in the past weeks," one of the pirates boasted from behind Michael. Leah looked up through her hair to see the man's face. When this was all over, she'd personally like to kick him in the balls. She'd remember what he looked like and if she got her chance later, she'd take it.

Michael regained her attention with a few well-placed swats to her ass and lower, on the edges of her pussy. That made her squirm and flood the fingers still rubbing her clit. Ty was certainly getting a handful. Leah wanted to die of embarrassment. Either that, or pleasure. Who knew being spanked in front of a room full of alien men and two eager Sons of Amber could make her this horny?

The fingers left her and Michael tossed her back to her feet so quickly, her head spun. She brushed hair out of her face with shaking fingers, her eyes glued to Michael's. His face nearly glowed with satisfaction. She'd done that. Her submission to him had put that look on his face and she reveled in that for just a quick moment. Michael placed one strong arm around her waist and pulled her close, nipping lightly at her nipple and tugging it taut with his teeth. The sensation made her tremble and reminded her of the predicament they were all in as the pirates hooted and called out encouragement. She felt heat rise to the surface of her skin as she blushed, probably just as Michael had intended. The man was an expert at getting her to respond in just the way he wanted. The thought should have annoyed her, but it didn't really. She'd do anything for Michael and she really didn't mind that he knew it.

"Now," he said in a voice the brooked no argument, "go sit on the table in front of my brother and spread your legs for him. Use your fingers to spread yourself. Show him your pussy."

She wanted to protest, but she also didn't want another spanking. Sitting on the hard table would be uncomfortable enough after just a few stinging swats of Michael's hand. She didn't want to disobey again and earn more. At least not right away.

Rubbing her sore cheek, Leah sat gingerly on the table, shifting around Ty, who didn't move to make her life easier. No, he sat there, making her brush against him and work around his muscular bulk, lifting her leg high in the air, over his lap. He surprised her by catching her calf in one big hand, coaxing her to place her foot on the edge of the table, then lifting her other foot to the same place on the opposite side. This position opened her wide, exposing both pussy and ass as he used his hands to spread her legs as wide as they'd go.

"She's a flexible little thing," Ty commented to

Michael, talking over her in a way that drove her crazy, but also made her hot.

"Use your fingers, Lilla," Michael reminded her. She balanced on one hand, leaning back slightly, using the other to hold open the outer lips so Ty could get a good view. All the pirates rapidly filling the space behind his chair were also getting a good show, she realized, but she knew Michael wouldn't let anyone touch her...without his permission. She wondered just how far he'd go in proving his worth among these alien pirates and how far he'd push her.

So far, everything he'd done and asked of her had only driven her arousal higher. She hadn't known she would ever engage in this sort of behavior, but it felt good. Better than good, if the sticky liquid flooding her pussy was any indication. She never knew she had exhibitionist tendencies, but then she'd led a pretty tame life since joining the military. The absence of men made sexual self-discovery a bit difficult at best.

She wobbled on her precarious perch and Ty covered her hand with his own. "It's all right, doll. I'll take over from here." She moved her hand back as Ty's large fingers began stroking up and down, around her pussy. He lingered on the sides of her clit, never quite touching as he dipped his blunt-tipped fingers into her well over and over. One, then two, then three fingers found their way up her channel, spiking her arousal higher as she pressed back against the hard table, squirming against the pleasure. "I bet she tastes sweet," Ty shocked a gasp from her as he winked. "Most human cunts do."

"Try her and find out, brother." Michael's off-hand permission stunned her, but the fire in his eyes when she looked over at him ignited a fire in her womb. He was enjoying every moment of this-her compliance with his wishes, her submission.

She held his gaze until Ty's lips closed over her clit, shocking her into a convulsive shudder that took her by surprise. The pirates laughed and cheered as Ty rode her through a small completion. She felt him licking at her cum, probing her hole with his tongue and stroking her clit as he ate her more thoroughly than she'd ever experienced. The man had talent.

Leah panted as Ty came up for air, his concentration seemingly total on her pussy as he inserted one finger from each of his hands into her channel. He tugged gently in opposite directions, perhaps to see how wide she'd go, perhaps to open her up for later. She had no idea, but she loved the sensation, creaming for him again and again as he spoke encouragement.

"She tastes good, brother. She has a sweet pussy and a hole wide enough for either of us-or both." A shiver took her at his startling words, but Ty only winked, his devilish expression telling her he was teasing. *Wasn't he?*

"What about her ass? What do you think of it?" Michael's lazy question didn't fool her. He was probably hard as a rock beneath the table, ready for action.

"I'm not sure. Let's see." With shocking speed, Ty rearranged her legs and had her off the table, twirled around to face it. Gently he pushed down between her shoulder blades until her torso lay on the table, her ass sticking up in the air between Ty and

Michael's chairs. Two very different male hands stroked her cheeks. Michael's touch was possessive, Ty's merely arousing.

Ty's hands moved, spreading her cheeks as she was pressed forward against the table. "Looks tight," he commented as Michael's fingers moved within the crevice to tease her.

"That can be remedied."

"Brothers, allow me to give you this." The pirate leader rolled something across the table at Michael. Leah couldn't see what it was, but when she looked up, she saw other human women already being fucked by the pirates all around. The leader of the group had a wench riding his cock as he sat in his chair and his second in command stood over another girl who lay writhing on the table as he rammed an impressive organ between her legs. Other women were being similarly used all over the large room. It was a full out orgy and Leah guessed she and the little show Michael was making of her was one of the main entertainment's.

She understood his plan all at once. In order to keep her safe from being jumped by every pirate in the room, he made damn sure they were all too hot to wait. He'd used her body and her reluctance to show it as a way to inflame the jits, letting them watch her be punished then pleasured until they found women of their own to take the edge off. Michael's slow and very public path to pleasure ensured that Leah was left to them-Michael and Ty alone-for as long as they proved good entertainment. Little did the jits know they'd tangled with a sexual master. Sons of Amber knew how to prolong

BIANCA D'ARC

pleasure. They were probably the most skilled males in all the universe at such things. The pirates would tire long before Michael ever ended this little show.

A tongue shocked her back to the moment. Ty, she guessed from the angle, was licking her ass! The thought should have disgusted her, but the sensations riding up her spine were anything but disgust. She felt an object-cold and wet-swirling through the juices of her pussy and upwards as Ty moved away. The object warmed as it spent time next to her skin, but it was definitely foreign.

She gasped as Michael's sure hand slid the hard thing partway into her ass. It was some kind of dildo, she guessed, or a plug. Yeah, it had to be a plug of some sort, intended to train her to take a cock back there.

She'd never thought of doing such a thing before, but suddenly she wanted to try whatever Michael wanted. He was the expert, after all. If he thought she'd enjoy taking a cock up her ass, she was willing to give it a try. He was her trusted guide on this journey of sexual discovery.

Michael leaned over her as his hand pushed the plug deeper, little by little. He breathed in her ear, whispering low as his chest brushed her bare back.

"Take it for me, baby. Push out and accept this. Accept me. Accept all that I am and all that I want of you."

His hot words fired her soul as the plug inched deeper. Michael pressed tight against her back, pushing her into the table, placing a bit of his weight on her, trapping her in his desire.

"That's good, sweetheart. So good. It'll be even

better when it's my cock up in there. Good and tight and a sweet, sweet burn." He eased up as she sucked in deep droughts of air. "Or maybe it'll be Ty's cock up your ass while I'm in your pussy. What do you think of that, Lilla?" His voice sounded louder now and she looked up to find the pirate leader's eyes riveted on her body as his muscles tightened and he shot his load into the pretty girl riding his cock.

Leah moaned as Michael played with the plug. It burned, creating sensations she'd never even guessed at before. It was strangely pleasurable, but mostly because of the pleasure it gave Michael. Her subservience was firing him higher, she could feel it in his touch and see it in his eyes. She'd never seen him so impassioned before unless it was in anger, but this wasn't anger at all. This was desire. Stark, brutal, steaming desire. For her.

The thought made her knees weak.

The plug in her bottom seemed to get bigger and she squeaked, unable to hold back her surprise. Michael chuckled low in her ear.

"This toy grows, Lilla. Every time you accept a new level of entry, it pushes you for more. Just like I will. Until you're mine in every sense-in every orifice-in every way."

"Master!" She gasped as the plug grew larger again. It seemed also to secrete some kind of lubricant that kept replenishing so she was never dry, never too uncomfortable.

"I like the sound of that," Michael growled, moving back to sit behind her, his hands never leaving the round planes of her butt. "Now come here and sit on my lap." His hands guided her gently, brooking no argument when she tried to ease down on his lap. The plug gave her pause, but Michael wouldn't let that stop him as he pushed down steadily on her waist until she was seated on one powerful thigh.

He had one arm casually draped around her shoulder, plucking at her nipple with a relaxed rhythm that did nothing to calm the escalating fire in her loins. Michael was playing with her, teaching her body how to respond to him and she liked it all too much. She could easily become his slave in truth if she weren't extremely careful, but that could wait. For now, she was enjoying his touch-and his orders-too much to complain about much of anything.

Chapter Nine

The pirate captain, Nik'ael Jetsurat, was finished with his woman for the moment and leaned back to appraise Mike. Sure, he was looking at the pretty picture Leah made on Mike's lap, but the Son of Amber knew the other warrior's eyes were assessing what he could see of the new man in his midst. Mike knew how to play this game. Don't give an inch and don't make trouble. As a Dom he was good at the first part. It was the second half of the equation he sometimes had problems with.

But his steadying influence was perched naked on his knee. Like nothing else, Leah's presence here warned him to keep his cool. He would do all he could to keep her safe, including swallow his pride. For her, he'd do anything.

"Your woman," Nik'ael gestured with a full mug of beer towards Leah. "Where'd you get her?"

Mike thought fast. "I came across her ship about a month ago. A luxury yacht, if you can believe it. She'd taken off on her own. Just this one and a co-pilot that I gave to a friend on the way. I thought I'd keep this one," he hoisted her a bit higher on his knee, setting her breasts to jiggling enticingly, "for myself. It's taken a while to train her and she still has lapses, but eventually I'll get her to obey."

"You like them submissive, then? It's not an easy road, brother." The pirate shook his head as if he knew of whence he spoke. Mike looked at the man with fresh eyes. This was a man who'd tried to dominate a woman and failed utterly. Out there somewhere was the woman who had bested this pirate chief. The idea gave Mike hope, for if a man had once known defeat, he would have either learned from it or remained foolish. This man looked like nobody's fool, though he struck Mike as an odd sort of pirate.

Mike picked up his mug of beer and drank, holding the other man's gaze. "It's the only road for me, Captain."

"It's like that, eh? I guess you wouldn't be willing to share her around then? Pity."

"Not until I've conquered her completely. Perhaps then, but not before."

The pirate captain laughed and drank deeply of his beer. "The mother goddess probably hates your guts, Mik. I hope you find it's worth Her damnation."

Mike shrugged. "For me there's no other way. It's just the way I'm made."

The jit leader leaned back in his chair. "I knew a set of brothers like you once. They came to no good end."

"I'll take my chances."

The pirate nodded and settled down to business. "So, why have you come to me?"

Mike set about explaining his need for fifty human women and they negotiated an arrangement where Nik'ael might supply the women for a hefty portion of the cut. Mike asked a few pointed questions, but the pirate was irritatingly circumspect about details. Only Leah's calming presence kept Mike's temper in check. Just by being there with him, she cemented the deal, allowing him to act like any other jit'suku pirate, interested only in profit and sex.

They talked business for about half a standard before they concluded their negotiations. The pirate would make his decision and let them know by the next morning if they were going to do business or not. Then he turned back to his slave girl and Mike got up to leave with Leah, inviting Ty to join them.

He'd gleaned a few important things from his conversation with the pirate captain. For one thing, jit women were scarce enough to create a high-paying market for human women. The why of it, he didn't know, but he'd find out. Somehow.

The pirate didn't even blink an eye when Mike said he wanted fifty women. The thought that this bastard might be used to sending even larger quantities of human women to the jit'suku home galaxy made Mike wince. This smuggling ring was much worse than he'd thought.

He also wondered why jit'suku women were so rare. From all reports before the war had started in earnest, jit'suku were much like humans in that about fifty percent of their population was male and roughly fifty percent female. Certainly the cultural differences were great, causing most jit women to stay on their home worlds with only the males venturing to the stars and making war on the Milky Way Galaxy.

Mike couldn't come right out and ask why women were suddenly such a rare commodity, though he'd sorely wanted to. The pirate leader's words had alluded to some great tragedy and Mike had a sneaking suspicion-based on mounting evidence-the jit civilization was in dire straits.

But he couldn't talk freely about any of this. Not yet. He knew they were most likely still being monitored. There was no help for it. They'd have to stay the night in this sector of the station, which would probably cause havoc on the legit side of the base. Smithson would be wondering where they were, trying to find them and figure out what they were inspecting incognito for so long. It would drive the woman crazy. Mike liked the idea of that-as long as she didn't figure out exactly where they were. He'd laid the groundwork before ever leaving Atlantia Station and contingency messages would be sent from his base that would send her searching for them in all the wrong directions.

They arrived back at the small compartment they'd used earlier and Mike motioned for Leah to precede him through the door. He couldn't keep his eyes off her pretty ass, plugged and primed, ready for him. Ty would be part of this, too. Mike had noted the way Ty's touch excited Leah when they'd played to the crowd. He wouldn't let Ty take her pussy-that was for Mike alone-but he'd let his brother participate in other ways. Ty probably needed relief as badly as he did, and Mike wanted to give this experience to Leah. Few human women even knew one lover in these dark days, much less two at once.

If any woman deserved all the pleasure he could bring her, it was Leah. She was the most important person in the universe to him and he'd keep her safe any way he could. For now, if keeping her safe-keeping their cover story in tact-meant showing her a pleasure she'd never had, so be it. She'd love it. He'd make certain of it.

* * * *

Leah walked gingerly into the small cabin. The plug wasn't exactly uncomfortable, but it was definitely strange. Michael's possessive gaze seared her skin and she schooled herself not to show too much alarm when Ty followed them into the compartment as if he belonged there. No doubt the jit pirates who were monitoring them expected both men to have her. The forbidden thought of such decadence sent a secret thrill up her spine. All she really needed was Michael, but she'd be lying if she said she didn't think Ty was gorgeous. She knew he liked her as well. He'd flirted and propositioned her so many times, it had become a joke between them, but she knew deep down, he truly admired her. Had her heart not been set on Michael from almost the first moment she met him, Ty would definitely have been on her "to do" list.

She chuckled inwardly, knowing the wickedness of her thoughts reflected in the sparkle of her eyes. Michael was watching her every move, searching her expression subtly, while Ty's gaze feasted on her body. Between the two, she counted herself a very lucky woman indeed.

"Get on the bed." Michael's commanding voice sent a shiver down her spine. She moved past him

toward the bed, yelping when his open palm
smacked her ass. "Get a move on, girl." Both men
chuckled as she scrambled onto the bed. "Hands and
knees, Lilla," Michael instructed. She moved quickly
to obey, feeling dreadfully exposed. She looked back
at the men over her shoulder, a little thrill going
through her as she caught the expressions of lust in
their eyes-focused on her. Who'd have believed it?

"She has a great ass." Ty licked his lips as she
watched, her own mouth going dry at the flare of
heat in her body.

"I'll let you have it later, but you aren't getting
any pussy. I'm trying to breed her." The bold
statement got Ty's attention, she saw. The men
shared a long, penetrating look before Ty nodded
and moved toward the head of the bed. She followed
his progress, feeling the heat of Michael as he took
his position behind her. His hands flowed over her
back and waist, down to the cheeks of her butt and
lower, over her thighs. His caresses brought a moan
to her throat as she closed her eyes in ecstasy.

"Eyes up, girl," Ty's voice came from just in front
of her. She opened her eyes to discover a long, thick,
hard cock positioned just in front of her. Ty. He
waited for her to look up, coaxing her with a finger
under her chin. His smile was pure deviltry as he
winked at her. "Lick me, sweetheart. I've been
dreaming of this."

"Do as he says." Michael's voice challenged her,
the Dominant tone exciting her even more.

Swallowing hard to gather her courage, Leah
bent her head the short distance needed to touch her
tongue to Ty's magnificent cock. She noted the slight

tremble of his limbs with satisfaction, but lost her train of thought when Ty pushed forward, invading her mouth at the same moment Michael tugged the plug from her bottom in one smooth motion.

The dual sensations made her gasp, but Michael soothed her with gentle hands on her bottom as Ty filled her mouth with a demanding hardness.

"She's good, Mik. With a little training, she'll be an expert."

A dark chuckle sounded from behind her.

"She's already come a long way, but I'm enjoying every minute of the process."

"I just bet you are." Ty dug his fingers into her hair. The move probably looked fierce to an observer, but his fingers were gentle as he coaxed her eyes to his. "You're beautiful, doll. Just keep doing that." She pulled strongly, holding his gaze. "Oh, yeah. Suck it, baby."

She was getting into a rhythm, coached by Ty's demanding hands in her hair, when Michael pushed into her with no warning. She was so ready, though, it didn't matter. He slid home with little fuss, causing the most delightful chills up and down her spine. The two men set to work then, one moving forward while the other retreated. She was being fucked on both ends with little to do except try to keep up.

She was on the verge of being completely overwhelmed by two Sons of Amber working in concert. One was more than enough for any woman, but to have two pleasuring her went beyond the realm of dreams. Her passion drew higher, into a place she had never quite reached before.

Ty came first, shooting down her throat. He

eased up, giving her a chance to breathe at the very last, but she took all he offered and finished him with stroking licks that made him grin. Then it was Michael's turn.

He powered into her, climaxing with a grunt that she'd never heard from him before. He splashed her womb with seed while Ty held her shoulders, helping her withstand the force of Michael's final thrusts as well as her own shuddering orgasm. Her arms went weak and only Ty saved her from flopping face-first onto the bed. He stroked her shoulders as she gasped, holding her close as he sat on the bed, cradling her head with his strong thighs.

Stuck between two lusty Sons of Amber was a position she'd remember fondly for the rest of her life.

* * * *

She collapsed on the bed, wrung out and asleep almost as soon as he moved to take her in his arms. Michael felt a pang in his heart as he held her, stroking her hair. This woman was so special to him. He'd liked giving her an experience few women knew these days, but at the same time he worried.

It was an unfamiliar sensation. Michael Amber seldom worried about anything, much less a woman's affections. More often, he was dodging unwanted declarations of undying love. This time, he worried about hearing just such words from Leah-for him alone. He realized with some shock he was actually jealous of Ty's role in bringing her to fulfillment. He wanted to reserve her cries of joy for his ears alone.

While he didn't begrudge his brother, or Leah, this moment out of time, he knew he didn't want to repeat it. But what if she did? What if he wasn't enough for her? That had him truly worried.

Ty caught his attention as he stood from the other side of the bed and shrugged into his clothes.

"You've got one hell of a woman there, Mik. Thanks for sharing."

"Anytime, my friend." The words were said carelessly, but the silent message in Michael's eyes was seen and understood as Ty nodded just once.

Mike wanted to talk to Ty about the conflict inside him. His brother would understand, if anyone. But they were still being monitored by the pirates and the mission had to come first.

"I'll leave you to her, then," Ty nodded at the unconscious woman in Mike's arms. "See you tomorrow."

With a parting wave, Ty left and Michael pulled the thin cover over Leah and himself, wrapping her in his arms. He held her through the night, lying awake for hours, contemplating the warm feel of her, the delicious taste of her skin, and the uncertainty of their future. Could he make a life for them together? Would she welcome the idea? It would be hard for a Son to take himself off the market, but a few of his brothers had done it. The question was, could he? He didn't know, but with Leah-for Leah-he'd like to try.

She meant more to him than anything, or anyone, in the universe. When this mission was over, he'd take the plunge. He wanted her in his life on a permanent basis. He wanted her tied to him with irrevocable bonds. He wanted her. Period.

Now the question remained to haunt his sleep-
did she want him in return?

Chapter Ten

Michael was sleeping soundly when Leah woke the next day. Unaccustomed to lying about when there was work to be done, she decided to do what she could for their mission. She doubted any of the pirates would give her trouble. Michael's ownership had been clearly established the night before.

Rummaging through the small closet quietly, she found some clothing to wear before peeping out into the hall. It was deserted, but she smelled the faint aroma of cooking food. That's where the women would probably be, considering the jits had specific gender roles and food preparation was firmly in the female realm of responsibility.

Following her nose, Leah was pleased when her scouting mission ended in a relatively large kitchen compartment where about a half dozen human women worked and talked quietly, preparing breakfast. One of them saw Leah standing in the doorway and beckoned her over.

"Fetching breakfast for your man?"

The woman's expression was friendly enough. Leah nodded, not sure what to say to these women. They seemed happy enough to be prisoners of the jit'suku, which struck her odd at first. But then, there were few human men left and there had always been women who reveled in being simply the companion and bedmate of a male. Leah didn't quite understand it herself, but she knew enough about human psychology to at least guess at what might motivate some of these women.

"I'm Lilla." She decided introductions might start the ball rolling.

"Nedda," said the woman while stirring a big pot of protein porridge the jits seemed to favor. "That's Julie," she pointed to a pregnant woman sitting at the table, "Billy Jo and Una are over there by the refrigeration unit, and Cassie and Kim are working on the bread."

"Is there anything I can do to help?" Her offer was met with a friendly smile as Nedda handed her a grinder and something that looked like a root.

"Hold that over the pot and grate this *snillet* until I say stop."

Leah did as she was told, gratified by the slightly cinnamon smell rising from the alien *snillet* as she ground it up into little slivers that fell into the porridge pot.

* * * *

Leah returned to the bedroom compartment about an hour later with breakfast and a great deal of information. She knew the smile on her face was smug, but she couldn't help herself. Michael would be proud of her, once she figured out how to convey her intell without alerting those who were undoubtedly monitoring them.

That might prove difficult, but she'd come this

far. She'd figure a way to drop it into the conversation.

"Where've you been?" Michael's harsh tone put a little damper on her spirits, but she wouldn't let him get to her.

"I got breakfast, Master."

Just that quick, the worry in his eyes changed to guarded observation. Slowly he nodded. "You may serve me."

She had to stop herself from laughing at his kingly tone and set about serving him breakfast in bed like the dictator he was pretending to be. His gaze followed her every move.

"Where did you get this food?"

"I found a kitchen where some of the other women were cooking breakfast for the group. I helped and they let me borrow the tray and utensils when I left. They're very nice, especially since most of them are here by choice."

"Unlike you?"

"No, Master," she was quick to answer as he pulled her down by one hand to sit on the side of the bed. "Like them, I started out as your prisoner, but now I want to stay. I like having a man in my life again. Truly." She was playing a part, but the love in the hand that rose to stroke down his shoulder to his chest was real. Still, she had to stay on track here. There was something Michael really needed to know. "Especially since all your jit women are dead. Don't you think it's fate? That the virus that killed all our males turned back on your people and killed your women?"

She felt Michael's muscles tense, but his

expression stayed cool. "Perhaps only fate could be so cruel," he said after some moments. His hand cupped the back of her neck and he pulled her in for a kiss. "You're a beautiful woman, Lilla, and an obedient slave. Sometimes."

He was teasing her. "But you like it when I disobey. Don't you, Master?"

He nodded, nibbling at her lips. "As much as you do, sweetheart."

She reveled in his kiss until her conscience stopped her. She had to tell him the rest. She pulled away just slightly. "I'm glad the mutated virus doesn't affect human women. I understand now why you captured me, Master. If I were a warrior, I'd have lassoed any man I could find when all of ours died. Your people are suffering, just like mine did, and I'm sorry for it."

"You have a compassionate heart, Lil."

* * * *

He'd be damned if Leah hadn't just handed him the biggest piece of intel he'd received thus far. Could it be true the jit virus had turned back on its creators? That would certainly be some kind of poetic justice, though a tragedy to be sure.

Mike worked hard to hide his racing thoughts. Kissing Leah was a good way to disguise his internal upset at the news of such staggering death in the jit'suku galaxy, but it was also distracting. He set her away and tried to smile.

"No time for that now, wench. I have work to do today." He slapped her curvy ass playfully as he rooted around for his clothes. She'd folded them and placed them on the room's only chair like a good little slave. Playing the part, he knew, but it felt kind of nice to have a woman care for his things. "Gather our stuff, we're heading out."

She buzzed around the small room, doing his bidding. They didn't have a lot of things with them, but it wouldn't do to leave anything behind. Leah was ready by the time he'd dressed. They ate together quickly and then headed out of the small compartment. Michael wasn't letting her out of his sight for a moment. Not now. Not ever.

He found the pirate leader in the same common room from the night before, eating breakfast. A few of his men were there as well, but most looked half-awake after a night of debauchery.

Michael sat opposite the captain and tried hard to repress his excitement. This op was nearing its conclusion. All he had to do now was finesse all the players into position. That would start now, with this man.

"I have some other business I need to attend to," Michael said. "Can you help me with the fifty or not?"

The captain sat back, eyeing him. Just when Michael was sure he'd overplayed his hand, the man dug out a crystal from his pocket and rolled it across the table.

"The information's on there. Coordinates, instructions for credit transfer, and everything else you'll need. Be ready tonight at seventeen hundred station time."

Mike thought fast. That would be cutting it

close, but it could be done. He had his troops on alert, waiting for his signal. He nodded to the jit captain.

"I'll be ready." Michael stood, noting Leah's warm presence behind him. "Thanks for your hospitality, Captain." He reached across the table to shake hands the way jits did—a bone-jarring elbow clasp—and quickly took his leave.

On the way out of the room he caught Ty's eye and with a silent signal, their plan went into motion. Michael knew Ty would be taking his leave of the pirates shortly, though he'd be monitoring their movements closely while the strike force prepared. As for the troops, Michael would take great pleasure in leading the team himself, though of course he'd be helmeted like all the other troopers, so it was likely the pirates wouldn't even recognize him.

He'd remember them, though. And he'd be on the lookout for certain particular devils he'd taken note of last night. Some of these men were worse than barbarians. They were downright cruel in the way they treated the women.

Mike knew they were being followed as they ducked into the access tubes that would bring them to the docking area. No doubt the pirates wanted to be certain just where their new contacts were going. Of course, he'd planned ahead. There was a small civilian craft waiting for them, which they used to their advantage. Mik and Leah got on the craft, greeting the specialist they'd assigned to this particular task, a veteran named Suzette. She was a crack pilot and something of an ace. She was also one of Leah's closest friends and a trusted member of the command staff.

Suzette looked them over as they entered the craft. One dark eyebrow arched and her sparkling eyes danced with humor, but she refrained from commenting on their appearance. She had a change of clothing waiting for them and they took turns in the ship's small necessary. Michael contacted his strike team through the secure comm while Leah changed.

After setting the wheels in motion, Michael went aft to change out of his pirate garb and into battle armor. He'd stripped down in the hall, not waiting for Leah to finish up in the even smaller sanitary compartment. He'd donned the lower portion of the battle suit, letting the sleeves of the flexible underskin hang around his waist while he fastened his boots and the armor plate that went over his legs. He heard the compartment door slide open and looked up to find Leah standing before him.

The sex kitten was well hidden under her starched battle dress uniform, but there was a knowing light in her gaze as it roved over his bare chest. He walked right up to her and cupped her cheek.

"It's good to have you back, Colonel. Not that I didn't enjoy Lilla." He winked and she laughed.

"It's good to be back, Commandant. And it's good to finally know what's going on in this sector." Michael nodded and stepped back, turning so she could help him with the sleeves. He could do it himself, but it'd be awkward, and soldiers often helped each other. Leah knew just what to do, setting to work dressing him with her usual efficiency. If he noticed the brush of her fingers over his skin more now than he ever had before, he supposed that was to be expected after the intimacy they'd shared.

Of course, they'd never gone into battle together before. All the time Leah had worked for him, he'd never taken her along on a mission where he knew he'd see fire. That she was here now was both troubling and uplifting. There was no other woman he wanted by his side, through thick or thin, but he couldn't find the words just yet to tell her. He didn't know how she'd respond and the uncertainty chipped away at his normal calm. Plus, there was a lot to get done tonight and in the coming days in this messed up sector of space. They had serious amounts of work to do and he didn't feel quite brave enough to broach the subject of the future and his uncomfortable feelings just yet.

First they had to clean up Smithson's mess and put an end to the slavery ring. Leah would play her part, as would he.

"I agree wholeheartedly. And even better," he turned back around to face her, "we finally have a reason to get rid of Smithson."

"You took a look at the data crystal then?"

"First thing. That...woman." He bit back the curse he would rather have used. "Is in this up to her eyeballs. She's the pirate contact. And the payment account is her very own."

"The bitch!"

Michael nodded. "You know what to do, Leah. I'm counting on you to get the station under control while I go after the pirates."

A steely light entered her eyes. "It will be my

pleasure. I've been wanting to kick Smithson's ass for quite a while now."

He leaned in to peck her cheek. "God, I love it when you're fierce."

She surprised him, placing both her hands around his neck and drawing him close. She cradled his head in her soft hands and looked deeply into his eyes.

"Be careful, Michael. I-" She swallowed hard. "I don't want to lose you."

"You won't ever lose me, Leah. I'll be careful, but you know I have to do this. I can I.D. the pirate leaders and do this part of the job more efficiently than anyone else. Trust me, I won't take any unnecessary chances. I'm a Dom, not a Risker like Ty."

* * * *

His lopsided smile melted her heart. "Thank heaven for that."

She bit back the cautions she wanted to voice. She knew he was a warrior of the highest caliber. He was one of-if not *the*-best. She shouldn't worry, but she did. Still, they both had tasks to perform. That he'd leave the station side of things in her hands was a matter of trust that was very flattering.

Sure, she knew she could handle anything Smithson could dish out, but for Michael to trust her with such a task indicated just how much he believed in her abilities. How much he trusted her to get the job done right. She had to trust him just as much. Still, it wouldn't prevent her from worrying...just a bit.

She reached up to kiss him one last time, then helped him on with the rest of his battle armor. His body would be well-protected behind layers of flexible armor. He'd be fighting the pirates while she conducted her own battle on the station.

He pressed a small data crystal into her hand. "Here's everything you need to arrest Smithson and her entire command staff. I want them all confined and separated until we can investigate and discover which of them were in it with her. I'm also giving you full authority to deal with anything on the station as you see fit. You'll be acting Commander in this sector until we can get someone else out here."

"Colonel," Suzette's voice piped in over the comm. "Your ride is here."

Leah clutched the crystal and gave Michael one last hug and kiss. They'd arranged for Suzette to pull away from the station and rendezvous with the troop carrier that held the strike force Michael would be leading. They'd docked with the larger ship and the small shuttle that would take Leah back to the military side of the station was now docking on the other side of the ship. Within a few minutes, Colonel Leah Blackfoot would be back in her domain, on the military side of the station, kicking butt.

"Give 'em hell, Leah." Michael winked at her.

"You too, Michael."

She left through the small hatch that would take her to the shuttle. She wanted to say more, but there was no time. And truth be told, she wasn't quite brave enough to tell Michael of her feelings. Not just yet. Maybe not ever.

She boarded the shuttle, drawing her mantle of authority around her like a protective shield. There was work to do. Hard work. She had to capture and confine a general and all her staff, and do it without giving any of them a chance to warn the jits of what was coming. Tricky business, but Leah had a plan, and several of her own people in key positions, ready to execute it.

Chapter Eleven

"Is your team in place, Tracey?" Leah spoke softly into the battle comm. They were communicating through shielded headsets on a coded frequency that only her group could access. None of the station personnel would know what hit them-if this went off as planned.

"We're ready when you are, Colonel." Tracey's quiet voice came back within moments.

So far, so good.

Leah straightened her spine and pressed the access panel that would open the command and control center's doors. She also had it rigged-courtesy of one of the women who were standing behind her, a wizard tech named Jane-to lockout all command functions the moment Leah entered the proper code.

She keyed it in. Immediately, all station systems would be locked down, waiting for her special override. It would only come when she had the station secure.

Once again she keyed the headset. "Go code Lima Bravo Foxtrot. Repeat. Lima Bravo Foxtrot. You have a go."

Just that easy, the plan was activated. Leah punched the door hatch and strode into the room, her team flanking her, their weapons at the ready.

General Smithson stood angrily from her command chair.

"What's the meaning of this, Colonel?"

"By authority of Sector Command, I hereby place you and your staff under arrest pending further investigation."

Smithson reached for her console, but Leah knew it was already deactivated. Any hope the woman had of erasing evidence or getting word out to her conspirators was long gone.

"You can't do this!"

Leah advanced, noting the rapid deployment of her squad of armed soldiers around the room.

"Kidnapping and turning a blind eye to the imprisonment and slavery of human women is a serious crime, General. I believe you should seek legal counsel before saying anything further."

"You bitch!" Smithson rushed her, but Leah was prepared. She hadn't had to call on her hand-to-hand fighting skills often, but she was no lightweight. She downed Smithson with one quick move, grabbing the woman's wrist as she tried to punch Leah in the face, and twirling her around into a prone position on the command deck. Leah held Smithson's arm out at an angle, one knee planted hard in her back, retaining control of the struggling woman. Leah looked up at the general's staff gathered all around, noting the expressions on each face carefully. Some were plotting, some simply stunned.

"You ladies can do this the hard way and end up like her," Leah chucked her chin toward the fallen woman, still struggling uselessly in her hold, "or you can go with my people quietly. We'll be questioning everyone and sorting out just who's involved in this despicable crime ring. If you've got nothing to hide, you'll be freed. As simple as that."

One by one, the wide-eyed ones stood, followed more reluctantly by the others. They filed out quietly, each put into restraints and escorted to the door by one of Leah's team. More of Leah's specially chosen troopers waited outside to take them to detention. The women of Smithson's command staff would be separated and questioned until Leah's people got to the bottom of the matter. Already, she had special investigators on site and more coming from Alantia Station. It had been a busy day, and it was about to get even busier as Leah and her team secured the station and restarted the computers, preserving evidence while getting on with the ordinary business of running the station.

She set to work, doggedly ignoring the impulse to check on how Michael's combat team was doing. They were on comm silence until their mission was secured and she wasn't going to be the one to break it, though she was tempted to report on her progress, just to hear Michael's voice. She had to trust him to stay safe and do his job...as much as he trusted her to do her part.

That thought in mind, she began the arduous work of documenting any possible mischief by Smithson's crew as she made decisions for every sector of the station. It was hard work, especially as they had to deal with ship crews unhappy with the station lockdown, but Leah wasn't letting anyone leave while Michael and his men were out there battling the pirates.

* * * *

Michael advanced into the jit areas of the station with his strikeforce. He wore full armor like the rest of the team, only his size and stature setting him apart from the female soldiers he commanded. He wore no insignia, nor did any of his troops. Coded comms delineated who was who among the helmeted, incognito warriors. Only they needed to know who was in charge, after all. Identifying the leaders to the enemy would only make them targets.

He enjoyed the adrenaline rush as he commanded the elite group of fighters. They were the best he'd ever worked with, and that was saying something. Many of them were smaller than him, but he knew beyond a doubt, they could more than handle a man of his size-or the jits for that matter. After some initial resistance, the pirates had been subdued with relative ease.

Ty-also in full armor that easily disguised his identity-sidled up next to Mike. To preserve Ty's cover, they'd arrested him along with the other pirates, then separated him out when they split up the pirates, with none the wiser.

"How are we doing, brother?" Ty asked on a private comm channel as he checked his weapons.

"We've got most of the main players, but can't seem to find the captain."

Ty's helmet bobbed as he nodded. "That's because he went back to his ship a few hours ago. Some kind of surprise inspection. He likes to pretend he's still military."

"Damn. Well, we'll get the captain when we take his ship. Everyone else has been rounded up and ferried out to our ship's holding cells. Just a few left here on the station. Comms reports no transmissions left the station." Michael nodded in satisfaction.

"Leah came through."

"I had no doubt she would. She's the most capable officer I've ever served with."

Ty pounded him on the shoulder. The armor took most of the friendly blow, but Michael still felt it. "Is that admiration I hear in your voice, Mike?"

He noted the teasing in his brother's voice, but refused to rise to the bait. They still had work to do. It was clear Leah was doing her part, now it was up to them not to let any of the pirates' slip away.

"Let's load our troops into the pirate shuttle and take their ship."

The plan had been hatched hours before. The pirates kept a troop shuttle nearby to transport them back and forth from their ship to the station. Ty had supplied the intelligence that most of the pirate crew was on the station at the moment, and it certainly looked like they'd rounded up most, if not all, of the command staff. With any luck, only a skeleton crew would be left on the pirate ship. When Mike and his crew arrived in the pirate shuttle, they'd swarm on board and take them by surprise. If all went as planned.

They left the cleanup to troops that had been selected especially for the mission of ferreting out the stragglers who hid in the bowels of the station. They were under Leah's command and would be reporting back to her from the moment Mike left the station.

The pirate shuttle was cramped, but the design would stand his team in good stead. Used for raiding parties, the shuttle had been equipped with quick-release hatches that allowed the maximum number of fighters off at one time. It would be relatively easy to board the pirate ship with this kind of equipment, and better yet, the crew left on board the pirate ship wouldn't realize, with any luck, that they were being boarded until the last possible minute.

Ty had secured the comm codes necessary to dock with the ship and all went off without a hitch, until they hit the hangar. Mike offloaded with the first group of troopers, only to meet heavy resistance. This was no skeleton crew.

It wasn't the full contingent of pirates, but this crew was more battle-ready than Mike would have liked. Apparently their captain routinely ordered any and all approaching shuttles to be greeted with maximum firepower, and this was no exception. The bloodthirsty bastards opened fire the moment they saw the battle armor. Their own crew wouldn't be armored and armed, ready for a fight.

Mike dropped to one knee, laying down suppression fire as best he could while his troopers swarmed around him, searching out covered positions. They leapfrogged their way across the hangar, suffering a few casualties, but nothing life-threatening thanks to their superior armor. Mike's own armor took a few hits, but he was leading the charge, in the thick of the fighting.

God, how he'd missed this!

Being in command was a deep-seated need, but there was something about putting your own life on the line that fired adrenaline like nobody's business. Mike had worked his way up, fighting and then leading as he learned and excelled. He hadn't been in combat in far too long. Not that he relished bloodshed, but he felt a sense of purpose on the battlefield that was all too often lost in the offices of command. Here he knew clearly who the good guys and the bad guys were.

In this case, the bad guys were jits. Kidnappers and slavers, these men were scum and Mike had no qualms about blowing them away when they tried to do the same to him.

* * * *

Leah sat in Smithson's old command chair, working steadily, when a comm interrupted on a private channel. Leah motioned her comm tech to record and punched the receive button.

"Where's Smithson?" The pirate captain looked angry. Very different from the over-the-top barbarian she'd met earlier. He didn't seem to recognize her at first-until she smiled. "You!"

"Colonel Leah Blackfoot of Sector Command." She nodded her head politely, while the pirate sat back, clearly shocked. "You're under arrest, Captain. You and your men are ordered to stand down immediately and surrender your ship to the forces already on board ."

The man stared at her for so long, she wasn't sure what he might do. Then he started to laugh, shaking his head as a grudging sort of respect entered his eyes.

"You're good, Lilla. Or should I say, *Colonel*? You had me fooled. I was scrutinizing the men when all along I should have suspected the girl. Damn, but you've got brass balls, woman!" Leah had to stifle a laugh. "What happened to Smithson?"

"She's currently enjoying the hospitality of the brig. I'd be delighted if you'd join her."

"A captain never surrenders his ship."

Leah watched the door behind the man open over the comm. She thought she recognized the big build of the two soldiers who entered first. It had to be Ty and Michael. The pirate captain saw them as he turned-too late to get off a shot.

"Looks like you don't need to surrender, Captain. You've been taken honorably in battle."

"You're a worthy adversary, Colonel." He bowed his head, surrendered his weapon, and spoke a few words in his own tongue she didn't quite follow as Michael and Ty cuffed him and passed him over to the waiting troopers.

One of the armored men stepped forward to face the screen and nodded as a transmission came through over the headset all members of the operation wore.

"We've secured the ship and will be heading back shortly." Michael's voice came through loud and clear. Leah had never felt so relieved. He was alive and sounded just as in control and strong as he always did, though his armor was blackened in places. He'd taken a few hits, but looked like he was moving all right to Leah's eyes.

"Glad to hear it, Commandant. We'll leave the light on for you."

BIANCA D'ARC

"Good work, Colonel." Did she hear a hint of pride in his voice? She wasn't sure, but the approval felt good. "We'll be there shortly. I'll meet you in Smithson's quarters. Bring your best evidence team. I want to see what we can learn from her belongings. If this crime ring goes any further, I want to know it. I'll also need a second evidence team to comb this ship for information."

They'd discussed this earlier and Leah knew Ty would be staying on board to help gather evidence from the pirate ship. He knew the codes and language of the jits better than anyone.

"Ready and waiting for your arrival, sir."

"You're the best, Leah. We'll see you in two standards."

* * * *

Michael met Leah in the hallway in front of Smithson's private quarters. There was a team of women behind her, or he would have dragged her into his arms for the homecoming kiss he really wanted. Aside from that, he was still in full armor and he wouldn't be able to enjoy her soft body against him as much as he wanted. No, the hug could wait until they were alone. For now.

She reached up to help him with the fastenings on his helmet without being asked and then they were face to face. There was so much he wanted to say, but he wasn't free to speak his mind. Not yet.

The moment would come soon. He'd had time to think while he was out on this mission, time to realize what was important and what wasn't. Leah.

195

She was what mattered most to him. She mattered more than any person he'd ever known, any woman he'd ever bedded, anyone, anywhere.

"Good to see you safely returned, sir." Her eyes spoke more than her words and Michael read every nuance.

"Good to be back. Are we ready, Colonel?"

"Yes, sir." She turned to the evidence team behind her, signaling them to begin recording. "Override codes, sir?"

Michael did his part, entering the command codes unique to him that allowed access to all parts of any station or base under his command. The doors to Smithson's private domain opened after a moment and specialized members of the evidence team entered first, lest the place be booby-trapped. When the initial guard called the all clear, Michael and Leah entered, observing as the team tapped into Smithson's personal files.

"Encrypted media here, sir, and lots of it," one of the techs called. Michael walked over to investigate while Leah continued to assist with the initial search of Smithson's personal effects.

"Box it all up for the experts, Ensign. I want everything about this search to be totally by the book." Michael noted the rows of encrypted data crystals. There was too much here to delve into now.

"I've got a cryptography team on standby in case she had anything encrypted more tightly than I give her credit for." Leah came up beside him, a comfortable, welcome presence at his side. Damn, she felt good there. Next to him, under him, astride him.

Michael squelched his wayward thoughts. Time enough for that later. For now, they had to oversee this critical gathering of evidence. There was no way he'd let Smithson slide through on a technicality. The case against her was going to be tighter than a drum.

Chapter Twelve

Two standards later, Michael and Leah finally retired from the room, leaving the techs to mop up the remnants under supervision of the ranking officer. The woman was good and Leah trusted her, which was enough for Michael. He had to get Leah alone. There was so much he wanted to say...and do.

She followed him into an empty guest chamber in the command section he'd reserved for their use. The door slid shut as he pulled her into his arms, armor and all. He couldn't wait to kiss her, to feel her under his palms.

"God, I've missed you." Michael muttered against her lips as he drew her in for a long, deep kiss. His tongue claimed her mouth, his body seeking the warmth of hers, but the blasted armor got in the way. When he could draw the strength, he pushed away a little. "Help me get this armor off, Leah. I need to feel you against me."

Her smile lit his world. "You won't get any argument there." She giggled like a carefree schoolgirl as their hands tangled, trying to remove the armor as quickly as possible and only prolonging the agony as they fumbled. He liked the sound of her laughter. There had been precious little laughter in both of their lives recently, and his heart felt good they could find it together. There was a lot he wanted to share with this special woman, if she'd only give him the chance.

The chance of a lifetime.

His hands stilled as his eyes searched her face. After a moment, she became aware of his scrutiny, her small hands stilling over his heart as she looked up at him. They'd managed to get the top part of the armor off at least.

"I haven't thanked you yet."

"For what?" Her voice was breathless.

"For the way you handled this mission." He pecked her lips. "Your cunning intellect." He kissed her brow. "And your beautiful submission." He breathed against her lips. "It was the greatest gift I have ever received."

When he let her up for air, she drew back to meet his eyes. Her expression was clouded, a small frown marring her lovely brow.

"You know I'd only do that for you, Michael, right? I never was promiscuous."

"I knew." He bent to kiss her cheeks. "It meant even more to me, knowing you did it for me and me alone."

"I'd do anything for you, Michael."

The sheer honesty in her voice made his heart contract as he stared down into her lovely eyes. She fidgeted under his scrutiny and he let her go, just a few inches. He couldn't bear to be parted more than that from her at the moment.

"As it stands," she looked away, "I'm glad the mission was a success. Aside from a few minor injuries, we came out of this clean and with solid evidence to hang Smithson and her cronies."

Mike allowed the change in subject, knowing there were still a few things that needed saying before the air was clear between them. He feared and anticipated the next few minutes with equal fervor. If she responded the way he hoped, he might just be the happiest man in the universe. If not, he didn't know what he'd do. Perhaps chain her to his bed until she agreed? The thought had some merit, but first he'd see how she took his proposal. He had to work up to it though.

"You were brilliant, Leah." His hands stroked her back, gentling her. "Ty's cover is intact and the pirates think you were the sole agent involved in infiltrating their ring. I couldn't have planned it better myself." A smacking kiss followed his words. "You're going to get a promotion out of this, I think."

"To be honest, I don't want it if it means I can't be your XO anymore." She took a deep breath. "I was ready to resign my commission, Michael. I'm only staying because of you."

His heart stuttered. Could he be hearing her right? Things were looking promising for his plans, but he wasn't taking anything for granted.

"You honestly think I'd let you go?" He pulled back to meet her eyes. "If anyone tried to take you from me at this point, they'd have one hell of a fight on their hands. Leah," he knelt before her, grasping her hands tightly. "Marry me."

She gasped. "Are you serious?" A smile bloomed over her lovely face, then dimmed slightly. "But-"

"But what? Leah, you know you can ask me anything. Don't go shy on me now." He stood, capturing her once more in his arms.

"Well," still she hesitated, her face coloring ever so slightly. "What about your, uh, duties? Can Sons even get married?"

He laughed, his fears calming. "A few of my brothers already have, so I don't see why not. I'll still have to make deposits to the fertility banks, but you're my woman, Leah. I only want you from now on."

"Oh, Michael." Tears gathered in her eyes and he took it as a good sign, though she still hadn't said yes.

"I never knew what love was until I met you. I've never said this before to anyone, but I love you, Leah, with all my heart." He drew one of her hands up between them, placing a kiss gallantly on the back of it. "Will you be mine? Marry me, work with me, let us raise our sons together? I need you more than I need my next breath, woman. Say yes and put me out of my misery." His hopes grew with each sharp intake of her breath, each tear that rolled down her soft cheeks.

"Yes, Michael. Yes!" She sobbed as she threw both arms around his neck, kissing his face with eager lips.

Within moments the rest of his armor was thrown off and Leah's clothes made a heap at the foot of the bed. They clung together, each refusing to let the other go far until Michael asserted his authority. He rolled them so she lay astride his hips and pushed gently at her shoulders until she sat up, sheathing him in her tight warmth.

"Ride me, woman."

"My, you're bossy." She smiled down at him as she undulated over his hips.

Michael smiled. "You love it, though. And you," uncharacteristically, he paused as if unsure, his gaze narrowing, "love me." She gasped as he tugged at her hips with his hands. "Don't you, Leah?"

"Yes, Michael." Her voice was sure, her eyes speaking volumes. "I love you with all my heart."

* * * *

Hours later, Michael stroked Leah's shoulder as they lay twined together in the big bed. They'd have to get dressed and see to the cleanup of the station in a few more minutes, but they'd do it side by side. As it would be now, forever. Michael still couldn't quite believe it.

"When we get back, I'll have to ask the elders if you can be inducted into the tribe."

Leah's voice startled him out of his thoughts and her words had him scrambling for meaning. His confusion must have been written on his face. She leaned up on one elbow to look at him.

"Blackfoot is more than my family name, you know. It's also the name of my tribe. I'm descended from a long line of warriors, and now by marrying me, you'll be joining their ranks." She leaned back, snuggling into his chest. "If the elders think you're worthy, of course, but I wouldn't worry about that." She chuckled and stroked his chest the way he liked.

"I can see I'm going to have to do some research. Just how does one join your tribe?"

"Well, there's a ceremony and a big celebration.

In the old days, the warriors-mostly men-would spend the day in games of skill while the women prepared a feast. Nowadays, with no men left in the tribe, the few women warriors usually compete, but it's much more low-key. The food is still plentiful though, and quite tasty. Then the medicine woman will say a few words and you'll be inducted. Come to think of it, she could marry us, too, if you don't mind a traditional ceremony. Our medicine woman is licensed to perform legal marriages, though it's been quite a number of years since she's been called upon to do so." Leah kissed his collarbone. "I think it would bring a lot of joy to all of them to see the old ways live on a little with us and our children. It would bring hope too. A new start for the tribe. What do you think?"

"I'd be honored to marry you in the traditional way, Leah. Bringing hope is what we Sons do, more than anything else. This'll just be a different way of doing it, but I'm all for discovering new things." He sipped from her lips, sealing the thought with a tender kiss.

* * * *

Weeks later, Michael and Leah met with her grandmother, the matriarch of her family, and one of the most powerful elders of the tribe. They'd taken precious leave time and traveled to Pacifica Tert, the planet on which Leah was born and where her family lived still. Michael had learned about the tribe in the intervening weeks, meeting with a few of the other elders who lived on stations and worlds roughly on their path to Pac Tert, as the natives called it. The tribe, it turned out, was spread over the galaxy, with thousands and thousands of members, though their numbers had been cut in half by the virus, just like every other human population.

Every elder looked at Michael with an appraising eye-something he was used to as a Son-but in an entirely non-sexual way. They evaluated his character, his strength, his will, and his suitability to join their tribe. They all held great respect for Leah, welcoming her as a long-lost daughter who'd become a hero in their eyes. He liked the way they interacted with her and cared for her comfort. Their hospitality was undeniable, as was their acceptance of him after their initial appraisal. Things had gone well, but the most important hurdle was yet to be jumped.

Leah's grandmother. Retired General Adelaide Blackfoot herself.

Michael had never really connected Leah to the famous woman in his mind. General Blackfoot was a legend among the space-going soldiers of the line. Michael had studied her strategies from the early parts of the war between humanity and the jit'suku when he'd still been under Dr. Amber's care. Now that he put two and two together, he realized Leah Blackfoot came from a long line of military commanders. Her grandmother wasn't the only famous Blackfoot general. Leah's father and brothers had acquitted themselves more than honorably in the ongoing war before succumbing to the alien virus. Losing them had been a fierce blow to humanity's forces, but the women picked up and soldiered on.

Leah herself had done so, even after the tragedy of losing her husband so young. His admiration for her only increased when he realized how much she'd lost and what her bloodlines must have instilled in her. More and more, he began to feel almost unworthy of her, but there was no way he could ever let her go.

The old woman was still spry, though well into her retirement. Her shrewd eyes made Michael feel like a young recruit as he was introduced to the living legend, Adelaide Blackfoot. He shook her hand respectfully, surprised by the strength of her gnarled grip. Leah hugged the old woman close, tears of genuine joy and affection in her lovely eyes.

"So you want to marry my girl, eh?" the general asked.

Michael nodded. "I do, ma'am."

Shrewd eyes studied him. "I've heard all about you Sons. I even had a little input when Amber Waithe suggested the project. I bet you didn't know you have Blackfoot DNA in you." She chuckled.

"I know little of my genetic origins, ma'am, but I'm intrigued to learn whatever you can tell me."

The old woman settled into her chair. "I'll tell you what I know, young man. Pour the tea, Leah," she directed her granddaughter to a tea service that had been laid out on the table. "I knew Amber Waithe when she was just an upstart geneticist with a brilliant idea. She wanted to combine the DNA of the best of humanity to come up with you Sons. Judging by the look of you and the stories of you and your brothers' exploits, she did a damn fine job of it, too."

"Thank you, ma'am. But how-?"

"How do I know where at least part of your DNA came from?" She cut him off with a knowing grin on her wrinkled face. "Because I'm the one who gave it to her." She sipped her tea, leaving him hanging while her eyes twinkled. "I'm not a Blackfoot by birth, you understand. I married in. My people were of another tribe, now mostly lost. When Amber came looking for warrior DNA, I gave her a sample of my husband's. I had his old hairbrush and it contained-according to Amber-enough hairs with root follicles to give her at least a little of his genetic code. I gave her my own DNA as well, since she wanted diverse samples to combine together. I don't know how much of it ended up in the final mix that created you, but I like to think we did our part and that something of my husband lives on in you and your brothers."

Michael was stunned as he sat back in the chair. Leah looked about the same as the old woman continued talking.

"It all comes full circle now, of course. The Great Spirit has seen fit to bring you back to the tribe, to renew and rejuvenate our dwindling numbers and hopes. I like it. It has a sense of destiny about it and a feeling of rightness. What say you?"

She sipped her tea in the silence that followed.

"I honestly don't know what to say, ma'am."

Leah looked worried though. "But what if-?"

"I thought you might worry." Adelaide leaned forward and tossed Leah a data pad she'd had hidden under a pillow at her side. "I commed Amber a few days ago and asked her if there would be any

206

complications. This is what she sent back."

Leah scanned the pad and her eyes widened, but she didn't speak. A moment later, she handed the datapad to him. Michael read the words, amazed by what he was seeing. Dr. Amber had run an analysis of his DNA against a sample of Leah's obtained from her service file. The bottom line conclusion was that they'd have healthy, happy offspring and weren't a close enough genetic match to make any difference.

Amber had also included a private message at the bottom for Michael, wishing them well.

"Now that's out of the way," Adelaide went on, "I'm pleased to welcome you to the family, Michael, and to the tribe."

Leah grasped his hand, squeezing tightly. "Thank you, grandmother."

* * * *

A week later, they were married in an elaborate ceremony and Michael was officially inducted into the tribe. A huge party followed at which he was astounded to find not only his superior officers, but Dr. Amber Waithe and the Leader of the Governing Council herself, Mathilde Gray. It was a high honor that such important women would come to witness their marriage.

They took a few minutes out of the party to present both bride and groom with Distinguished Service Medals for their work in busting up the piracy ring in Smithson's sector. Leader Gray spoke glowing words about them both, much to the crowd's delight. Most of the tribe came to the wedding from planets near and far, summoned by the elders to witness what they were touting as the rebirth of their people. It was a heavy load to bear, but Leah handled it well. Michael was used to the pressure of having most of humanity depend on him for one thing or another, but this was slightly different. This was somehow more intimate. He was no longer just another of the Sons, but Michael Amber, husband to Leah Blackfoot-Amber, the first male to marry into the tribe since the virus struck.

It was a new beginning in many different ways.

"To the newlyweds," Leader Gray toasted them as they gathered for dinner in the formal dining hall that had been decorated by the tribal community in garlands and shimmering beadwork tapestries. "May they live long, healthy, fruitful lives, serving both the Blackfoot people and all of humanity."

A chorus of answering wishes rose from the assembly as they raised their glasses over and over. Michael rose, taking the occasion to put into words the feelings he'd never been good at discussing. Now was the time to let the women in his life know what he felt. Plus, the alcohol he'd already consumed helped loosen his tongue.

"I'd like to thank Dr. Amber Waithe." Michael spoke into the silence, raising his glass toward the scientist who'd designed him. "We call ourselves her Sons, but in every way that really matters, she truly is our mother. Thank you for being here to witness my marriage. Your presence means more than you can know." The woman teared up, smiling lovingly at Michael as he paused to recognize her.

"Thanks also to Leader Gray and those members

of the Governing Council and the chain of command who came all this way to join our celebration. Leah and I have lived much of our lives in the service. The military is our family as well and we're proud to have you here and have your blessing as we join our lives together." Murmurs of agreement sounded as the many uniformed officers and politicians in stylish suits bowed their heads or nodded and smiled in approval of his heartfelt words. But Michael wasn't finished.

"And thanks to my new wife, my heart, Leah." He turned to her, seated beside him, looking up with love in her eyes. She'd declared her love for him, but he hadn't reciprocated. Not in so many words. "I didn't know love until I met you, Leah. You've taught me so much I never imagined about being human. I value you as my best friend, the other half of my soul and the best damn Executive Officer I've ever had. I fully expect you to run the rest of my life as efficiently as you've run my command these past years." The crowd chuckled as he'd intended. He reached down and raised Leah by one hand until she stood at his side, gazing up at him. "I love you, Leah, with all my heart and forevermore."

He tugged on her hand until she was in his arms, his lips on hers as the crowd sighed. He kissed her with all the love in his heart, glad to finally be able to articulate at least some of the amazing feelings coursing through him. He tasted the salt of Leah's tears and broke off, folding one of her hands against his heart as he gazed into her weepy eyes.

"I'm glad you said that, Michael, because I love you, too." She breathed deep to try to control her tears, but the smile on her face was full of joy. "And I have something to tell everyone, too." A little devil of mischief entered her twinkling eyes. She squeezed his hand, holding his gaze as she spoke outward in a strong voice, to the assembly. "I'm pregnant."

Cheers erupted along with a flurry of congratulations. Everyone drank to the toast, but Leah's crystal flute of champagne was quickly replaced with a glass of water as she laughed at the fuss everyone made. Michael couldn't let go of her hand. He'd made many women pregnant, but never his chosen life-mate, the miraculous woman who'd brought him into her family, her tribe, her life. He'd never belonged before-not the way he belonged now. Michael felt as if he'd finally found his place in the human race. He'd found a family to belong to, and suddenly the future generations seemed much closer than they had before. Michael looked forward to raising this child, and any others they might have together.

The soldier Son of Amber had finally found a home.

About the Author

A life-long martial arts enthusiast, **Bianca D'Arc** enjoys a number of hobbies and interests that keep her busy and entertained such as playing the guitar, shopping, painting, shopping, skiing, shopping, road trips, and did we say shopping? A bargain hunter through and through, Bianca loves the thrill of the hunt for that excellent price on quality items, though she's hardly a fashionista. She likes nothing better than curling up by the fire with a good book, or better yet, by the computer, writing a good book.

Learn more about Bianca D'Arc and her books at www.biancadarc.com or read Bianca's blog at http://biancadarc.com/blog.

An Excerpt from
King of Swords
By Bianca D'Arc

Part of the *Fortune's Fool* Anthology
Available at Phaze.com

Set in the same future as the Sons of Amber, *but earlier in the timeline,* King of Swords *takes place a generation or two before* Ezekiel, *when the ongoing Rim skirmishes with forces of the jit'suku empire make the civilian stations in the outlying areas of the Milky Way Galaxy dangerous places to live.*

Adele pushed through the portal and waited a moment for her eyes to adjust to the gloom inside. What she could see of the place was clean and well kept. The atmosphere was dark, quiet and relaxing rather than sinister as she'd half expected. She noted the big men at the bar as her eyes adjusted slowly, scanning the room for her aunt. The place was set up with small private booths and one long bar area where the men clustered. Soldiers, they had to be, though they were all in civ clothing. On leave or perhaps retirees, she guessed, noting the bartender looked to built on the same grand scale. Soldiers were just bigger than regular human males. It had something to do with their diet and training, she knew, but other than that, she hadn't paid much attention.

Unlike many civilians, Adele had no real opinion about soldiers. Oh, she appreciated the sacrifices they made trying to keep the Milky Way Galaxy safe from the jit'suku threat, but she'd never really had any dealings with them on a personal basis. She knew many civ men discriminated against them-probably because they felt small by comparison.

She'd seen soldiers here and there throughout her travels and to a man they were all huge and rather intimidating. She supposed a civilian man would feel a little threatened by their towering height and imposing brawn, but she felt somehow comforted by their large, protective presence. Surely, if men such as these were fighting the jit'suku out on the rim, the rest of humanity would always be safe. They inspired that kind of confidence with their silent, somewhat menacing ways.

Adele swept the room once again but didn't see her aunt, so she decided to brave the quiet crowd at the bar to ask. She walked to an open space, feeling enclosed by the heat of the big men sitting on either side of her, but she refused to acknowledge the sort of tingly reaction that skittered through her body. It wasn't fear exactly, but it was definitely something that surprised her.

"Pardon me," she said in a voice that carried to the bartender. All eyes turned to her and she found herself the unexpected center of attention. "Can you tell me if Della Senna is here? I understand she's dealing here now." The bartender slung a towel over his shoulder and walked toward her with a rolling gait that oozed sex appeal. She'd never been this close to a soldier, much less half a dozen of them, and each and every one was solidly built, and handsome as sin. This bartender was perhaps the prettiest of the bunch, with perfectly chiseled features and a confident, friendly expression.

When he smiled, she felt the bottom fall out of her stomach. He was definitely what her old friend Mary would label DDG -- Drop Dead Gorgeous.

"Della's on break, but she'll be back in about five minutes if you want to wait."

His deep voice sent little shivers down her spine. The man was sexy as hell and dangerous to boot. She could feel it crackling in the air around him as he stopped right in front of her on the other side of the bar. She was glad of the hard metal of the bar between them. His attention shifted to the man seated on her right. A slight nod and narrowing of his eyes was all that was needed to make the other man jump into action. A moment later, he'd drawn a barstool up behind her and politely assisted her to sit.

"Thank you." She looked over at the man on the right, surprised by his youth. This soldier was definitely younger than her and his clothes looked brand new. Perhaps he was on leave. She smiled at him and his face seemed to heat just the tiniest bit with a flush of embarrassment. She liked the young man immediately. He was polite and a little shy, which surprised her even more. Built like a freighter, she wouldn't have imagined anything as simple as a smile could fluster him, but apparently it did.

"What'll you have, ma'am?" The bartender polished a small glass and set it before her, probably assuming she'd have a typical girly drink suited to the petite glass. Feeling daring, she smiled with an air of challenge. "Do you have any Pearson's Star Ale on tap?"

The bartender straightened and smiled, taking the little glass away. "Indeed I do. Coming right up."

When he turned to fetch her ale, she was treated to a lovely view of his sculpted ass. The man was pure muscle and his formfitting pants showed his assets off to best advantage. She'd bet he made great tips from the ladies based just on his butt alone. Sighing, she sat back on the surprisingly comfortable stool. She didn't feel as out of place here as she'd feared. The atmosphere was quiet, but welcoming.

A moment later the handsome bartender was back, placing a frothy, frosted pint before her with relish. Adele licked her lips, staring at the perfectly poured portion. She had a taste for this particular brew and didn't partake of it often due to its hefty price, but this occasion seemed to call for it. With relish, she took a sip of the thick, dark ale and the taste exploded on her tongue.

"Mmm, delicious."

She moved to get her credit chit, but a big hand swooped in from the side, pressing a credit chit into the bartender's hand.

"Allow me, ma'am."

Startled, she looked over to acknowledge the

huge man sitting to her left. Blonde and blue eyed, this guy was a little older than her. Probably a retiree, and a recent one, if the newness of his clothing was anything to go by. Soldiers didn't usually have a lot of money to spare when they left the service and this ale was a luxury. She couldn't let him pay for it in good conscience, though it was a lovely gesture.

"That's very kind of you but—"

"It would be my pleasure. My name is David." His smile totally disarmed her. It was even more devastating than the bartender's.

"I'm Adele," she found herself answering, though she hadn't intended to give out any personal information to people she didn't know on this little sojourn to the far side of the station.

"A beautiful name for a beautiful lady."

The bartender groaned. "You need to brush up your lines, Dave. That one's as old as the core." The other men around them laughed and David smiled good -naturedly. He seemed used to the ribbing from his comrades and paid it no mind.

"Doesn't make it any less true." His gaze held hers and for a moment it felt like only the two of them existed in the whole universe.

TAKE A FEW HOT
FANTASIES TO BED

PHAZE Presents ...

Fantasies
volume I

four tales of erotic romance by ...

**Alessia Brio
Leigh Ellwood
Bridget Midway
Ann Regentin**

Presents ...

ntasies
volume II

of erotic romance by ...

**Will Belegon
Petula Caesar
Sarah Dickson
Stella & Audra Price**

PHAZE Presents ...

Fantasies
volume III

tales of homoerotic romance by

**ames Buchanan
Jade Falconer
Eliza Gayle
Jamie Hill
Selah March
Yeva Wiest**

PHAZE Presents

Fantasies
volume IV

four tales of erotic romance by ...

**Vivien Dean
Eva Gale
Philippa Grey-Gerou
Cat Johnson**

Presents ...

ntasies
volume V

of erotic romance by ...

**ictoria Blisse
L.E. Bryce
Kate Burns
Emma Wildes**

PHAZE Presents ...

Fantasies
volume VI

tales of erotic romance by ...

**Yvette Hines
Augusta Li
Jude Mason
Derek Musgrave
Jessie Verino
and JN**

PHAZE SUPPORTS
EROTIC ALTRUISM

CPSIA information can be obtained at www.ICGtesting.com
Printed in the USA
LVOW082306211012

303826LV00001B/32/P